"S...

Jason's voice ... the hall light th... ...as strained. Alarm sharpened her tired brain. Had his father had another seizure? His next words belied the notion, and she sagged with relief.

"It's not safe for a woman to walk alone here after dark!" he raged.

She couldn't ignore his shouting and retorted, "Compared to Vancouver, Athens is as safe as the inside of a house. Besides, why should you worry? If something happened to me, you'd be free."

A strange expression flitted across his face and was gone too quickly for her to interpret. His midnight-blue eyes studied her with unnerving intentness. "That depends on your idea of freedom...."

Dear Reader:

SILHOUETTE DESIRE is an exciting new line of contemporary romances from Silhouette Books. During the past year, many Silhouette readers have written in telling us what other types of stories they'd like to read from Silhouette, and we've kept these comments and suggestions in mind in developing SILHOUETTE DESIRE.

DESIREs feature all of the elements you like to see in a romance, plus a more sensual, provocative story. So if you want to experience all the excitement, passion and joy of falling in love, then SILHOUETTE DESIRE is for you.

For more details write to:

Jane Nicholls
Silhouette Books
PO Box 236
Thornton Road
Croydon
Surrey CR9 3RU

FREDA VASILOS
Moon Madness

Silhouette Desire

Originally Published by Silhouette Books
division of
Harlequin Enterprises Ltd.

First published in Great Britain 1986
by Silhouette Books, 15–16 Brook's Mews, London W1A 1DR

© Freda Vasilopoulos 1985

Silhouette, Silhouette Desire and Colophon are Trade Marks of Harlequin Enterprises B.V.

ISBN 0 373 05231 6

22–0286

Made and printed in Great Britain for
Mills & Boon Ltd by
Richard Clay (The Chaucer Press) Ltd,
Bungay, Suffolk

FREDA VASILOS

has been married for fourteen years to a genuine Greek who bears little resemblance to the heroes of early romance novels set in Greece. She decided to write a book that would change readers' misconceptions about Greek heroes. Greek men are gorgeous!

For further information about
Silhouette Books please write to:

Jane Nicholls
Silhouette Books
PO Box 236
Thornton Road
Croydon
Surrey CR9 3RU

To John, my husband,
who believed in me,
and to Mary,
who believed in my work.

One

She stood on the sidewalk outside the house, a tall, slender young woman in an elegant blue silk dress. The high gates in the garden wall were open, but this didn't guarantee her welcome, she knew. They were seldom locked except at night, and darkness was only now falling softly about her. The house was even more beautiful than she remembered, the luxurious Kifissia residence of Jason Stephanou, the millionaire industrialist— *wasn't that how the magazines termed it?* she mused. A wry smile curled her mouth, briefly erasing the worry from her eyes.

Sophie's head was whirling with exhaustion after the long flight from Vancouver to Athens, but renewed anxiety brought out a clammy sweat on her palms. She rubbed them together, shivering slightly, though the evening was not much cooler than the hot August day had been. Her mind went back over the last three hectic days, which had upset the painfully acquired tranquility of her life.

Come at once. Father ill.

The terse wording of the telegram had been almost identical to one summoning her to Vancouver nearly two years before, only this one concerned her father-in-law, not her natural father. But her ties to Stavros were nearly as strong as those that had bound her to her own father. During the brief year of her marriage, she had grown to love her father-in-law—even as she had grown increasingly distant from Jason, her husband.

Apprehension sent another shiver through her. The nagging suspicion that Jason had sent the telegram hadn't left her these past three days. Could he have used this pretext to call her back to his sphere of influence? She'd left him because of her father's illness, but then she had stayed away, unable to return to the marriage that made a mockery of all her expectations of love.

Would Jason, with his arrogant Greek mind, forgive what must have seemed an act of defiance? Sophie considered herself, by birth and upbringing, to be completely Canadian, but her Greek father had imparted a sharp comprehension of his country's ancestral customs and conventions. Greeks were proud and possessed long memories. She could not escape the fact that she and Jason were still husband and wife.

She decided it was futile to attempt to analyze the complexities of Jason's mind on the sidewalk in front of his house, so with a determined set to her chin, she picked up her suitcase and overnight bag. Shutting her mind to doubts about her welcome, she quickly rang the doorbell.

Before its echoes faded she heard footsteps approaching, and in a moment the door opened, revealing Voula, the Stephanou housekeeper. Her incredulous start of amazement confirmed Sophie's suspicions about the telegram. She was not expected.

Voula enfolded Sophie in a warm embrace that started tears burning at the backs of her eyes. Expected or not, she was welcome. She had come home, really home.

"Sophie, you're back," Voula cried happily, closing the door as Sophie stepped into the foyer of the house.

"How is Stavros?" Sophie asked anxiously. She effortlessly made the transition from English to Greek.

"Stavros?" the housekeeper repeated, puzzlement clouding her brow. Then her face cleared. "He's all right now. He had a little attack a few days ago, but as long as he takes his medicine, it's nothing." Her fine dark eyes studied Sophie keenly. "He's an old man, Sophie. He missed you after you left. He'll be so happy to see you."

Sophie had a sense of plunging downward in a runaway elevator. "You mean he hasn't been seriously ill?"

"Not seriously, no," Voula said. "It's his heart. He's had minor seizures several times in the last year. If only he would remember to take his medicine." She took the suitcase from Sophie's unresisting fingers. "You'll be able to remind him."

"But I received a message," Sophie insisted, desperately trying to think. It must have been from Jason. If only her head were clearer—

She laid her hand on Voula's arm. "How many of the family are here?" she asked, unable to voice aloud the question that burned within her: *Is Jason here?*

"Only Stavros and Paul, and a male nurse Jason engaged for Stavros a few days ago to get him over this attack."

"So Jason isn't here," whispered Sophie.

Voula eyed her with a certain sympathy. In Greece, servants were often treated more like members of the family than hired help, and this household was no exception. "He's gone to Corinth for a couple of days on business."

Sophie's shoulders sagged in relief. A slight reprieve, but would it be long enough for her to arm her defenses? Corinth was only a matter of eighty kilometers away; the way Jason drove his silver-gray Jaguar, he could be home in less than two hours once he heard of her arrival. But now she had the advantage of knowing with certainty that he had sent for her, and it wasn't likely that only concern for Stavros had motivated him.

After two years of ignoring her existence, why did he suddenly want her presence in his house?

At that moment Stavros himself came out of the dining room. He looked much as she remembered him, his thick white hair springing vitally from his lean forehead, the brilliance of his blue eyes undimmed by time. He was perhaps a little thinner, a little worn, but he looked remarkably fit for a man she had feared to find on his deathbed.

"Sophie, my dear." He embraced her, kissing her enthusiastically on either cheek. "It's about time you came home."

Sophie swallowed hard before the lump in her throat would allow her to speak. Her legs were rubbery, threatening to give way under her. "I thought you were ill, *Patera*. I'm glad you're looking so well.'' At his request she had always addressed him by the formal title of ''father.''

Stavros shrugged in a typically Greek way. ''Just a little setback. As you can see, I'm recovered. Jason was unnecessarily alarmed.''

Sophie's mind cleared momentarily, and her eyes narrowed thoughtfully. Had Stavros known of the message? Perhaps even been party to it? He was a strong-willed man whose faculties had in no way dulled with age, and he had made no secret of the fact that he thought her the ideal wife for his tempestuous elder son. The idea dismayed her. With the two of them working together, what chance did she have of avoiding the web that was drawing her inexorably back into the family circle?

She became aware that Stavros was watching her strangely. She smiled at him without malice. Whatever he had done was motivated only by the best intentions. ''I'm sorry,'' she said. ''I'm just tired. It was a long flight.''

Stavros took her hand firmly under his arm. ''Come along. You must meet Paul and have something to eat.''

Paul was a younger edition of Jason, with similar features, but she knew in an instant that he lacked the drive and single-minded determination that had taken Jason from a poverty-stricken beginning in a remote Peloponnese village to being a millionaire in control of an international corporation. She had met Paul briefly at the wedding, but barely remembered him. He had only been granted a twenty-four-hour leave from the army to attend the festivities. By the time he had completed his tour of duty, she had already left Jason.

She felt his green eyes watching her speculatively as she tried to eat a little of the food Stavros pressed on her. Paul was about her own age of twenty-four, twelve years younger than Jason. Unlike his brother, he had known little deprivation in his childhood. His pleasant, open expression was in direct contrast to Jason's unyielding toughness. She sensed that Paul would be willing to be friends with her, and she was glad, as the day might yet come when she would need a friend to protect her from Jason.

It was late by the time Sophie was able to excuse herself. Stavros and Paul had wanted to hear all about her activities of the past two years. They only let her go when her fatigue became so obvious that even in their enthusiasm at seeing her again, they were forced to take pity on her.

Voula took her upstairs. Sophie knew immediately where the housekeeper had put her things—in the room that had been hers and Jason's, which she assumed Jason still used. This last was confirmed the moment she entered the door; his blue velour robe hung behind the door, and the hairbrushes she had given him the first Christmas they had spent together lay on the dressing table.

"Voula," she said in consternation, "I can't sleep here."

Voula's dark eyes were filled with sympathy, but she slowly shook her head. "All the other rooms are occupied. Besides, Jason won't be back for a few days. Tomorrow we'll see what other arrangements can be made."

Sophie had to be satisfied with that. Her fatigue weighed heavily on her, dulling her thought processes, and she found herself unable to argue further, wishing only to fall into bed and sleep forever. Perhaps when she awoke she would find herself back in Vancouver, living a quiet, orderly life divided between her shop and her comfortable apartment, where she had contentment if not exactly happiness.

She undressed and went into the bathroom that adjoined the bedroom. Mechanically she began applying cream to her face. Her skin, smooth and creamy over the classic bone structure of her face, was the envy of her friends, but Sophie took her beauty for granted. Her well-groomed appearance and the candid clarity of her gray eyes gave others an impression of a self-contained young woman who knew her own mind. Only she knew that her coolly elegant exterior often masked inner sorrow and uncertainty.

At first she slept soundly; then she became restless, tossing from side to side on the pillows. In a state midway between waking and sleeping she saw Jason—Jason with his hard, handsome face and his lean, graceful body. As had happened all too often in the last months of their marriage, he was shouting at her.

"How could you have bought this garbage?" he demanded, *lifting each of the framed paintings she had brought home and tossing them aside.*

"Helen says the artist has merit, that someday he'll be famous. It's an investment," Sophie said reasonably, *although her temper was rising.*

"How much did you pay for them?"

Silently, biting her lip to contain her resentment, she handed him the receipt.

"Thirty thousand drachmas *each, for three pictures?"* He seemed almost to choke with rage. *"Have you taken a good look at them?"* He thrust one under her nose. *"This type of thing is common on every street corner. What's this painter got on you?"* He paused, then a new thought struck him. *"Or are you in love with him?"*

"No," Sophie retorted, staring into his angry face. *"Helen said—"* Miserably, she trailed off. *Now that she saw the pictures clearly, without the artist's compelling sales pitch, she saw that they were mediocre, ordinary scenes of Greek islands like those available in every tourist shop in Athens.*

"'Helen said'!" he snorted in disgust. *"Don't you have a mind of your own, Sophie? It's my money you're spending so foolishly. Helen's monthly income would keep the average Greek family for a year. I'm not yet in the financial bracket where I can afford to subsidize every artist who talks persuasively."*

Sophie lifted her chin. "Then next time I'll use my own money."

This only angered him further. "Sophie," he said through gritted teeth, "stop acting like a spoiled child. You are my wife. You will live on my money. Just forget that your father could probably buy me out." He glared at her, and if looks could kill she would have disintegrated on the spot. Then he added as if he were thinking out loud, "At the moment. It won't always be like that."

With a start Sophie came to complete wakefulness, her eyes sweeping the room as if she expected to see Jason in the flesh. For a moment she didn't recognize her surroundings, then memory flooded back. This was Jason's room, Jason's bed.

That dream! Or was it a dream? She shook her head, blond hair swinging about her shoulders. It had happened, if not exactly like the dream. She had done many foolish things, childish acts to get Jason's attention.

His involvement with business had been such that she had seen little of him, and they had rarely gone out together except for business dinners and parties. After being the center of her father's existence throughout her childhood and adolescence, Sophie had expected the husband who had wooed her with amazingly romantic persistence and ardor to continue to indulge her every whim. When he began to resume his arduous workload soon after their honeymoon, she had been jarred out of her self-centered little world, becoming at first petulant and then, when this had little effect on Jason, angry. She had found small ways to get back at him, like buying the worthless paintings or shopping for extravagant clothes she never wore.

How young she had been! And how very foolish.

She sighed, sitting up in bed, wide awake since her inner clock was still on Vancouver time. Throwing aside the single sheet that covered her, she got up and walked to the window, ethereal in her long white nightdress, a creature of the moon. Drawing aside the curtains, she stepped out on the narrow balcony. The garden lay silver and blue in the moonlight, the heavy scent of the roses a narcotic that seeped into her mind, drugging it into forgetfulness. In a velvet sky the pale moon sailed serenely, reminding Sophie of another night when she and Jason had just been married. They had sneaked out of the beach hotel and gone swimming naked in a warm sea phosphorescent with moonlight, making love afterward in sand softer and more sensuous than any bed.

Had she really been so innocent and trustful of Jason? It was hard to imagine now.

A night bird called plaintively, and she returned to the present. How beautiful Greece was. Despite remembered pain, she felt welcome here. Even in the taxi coming from the airport, the heat and noise of the city had wrapped her with familiarity. And the first glimpse of the Acropolis had made her wonder how she had contemplated never returning to the city from which her ancestors had sprung.

Was that why she had come, even in the face of her apprehensions about Jason? Had the sea, the sun and the indelible memories called her?

With a deep sigh she turned back into the room, closing the shutters and banishing the treacherous moonlight.

Again Jason came to her, but a different Jason. He was smiling that peculiarly sweet smile strangers never saw, and his voice was seduction itself as it had been during their short courtship and their ecstatic honeymoon. Sophie reached out her hands to him to pull him close.

"Jason," she murmured longingly, lovingly.

His mouth touched hers in a tender kiss that sent the blood singing along her veins. Jason loved her and wanted her back. His warm hands stroked her body, effortlessly removing her clothes, and he laughed that she should wear anything to bed when he would only take it off.

"Jason," she sighed, and the sigh became a gasp of pleasure as he caressed her thighs with ravishing sensuality. Straining toward him, she gave a breathless cry

*that seemed to embody all her longing. "Jason, Jason,
love me. Oh, love me."*

*His voice was rough with his own desire, a tender
growl in his throat. "Yes, my darling, yes."*

*Her fingers dug into the hard muscles of his back as
he bent over her; then he was inside her, filling her, com-
pleting her, the two of them blending into a single enti-
ty. She cried out with a mindless, rapturous ecstasy—*

And awoke.

For a long moment she lay bemused. How real it had
been; yet the bed was empty beside her. The throbbing
pulse deep inside her gradually subsided, and she was
inexplicably filled with hazy contentment, as if some
long-endured tension had snapped. Like a tired child,
she turned her face into the pillow and slept once more.

Sophie awoke when the morning was already in full
bloom. Someone had been in the room; the shutters were
open, letting golden sunlight flood the floor and the bed,
the light breeze that gently moved the curtains bringing
in the sweet scent of roses. In the light of morning the
aroma held no seductive danger, only a warm essence of
summer. A thermos of coffee stood beside a delicate
china cup and saucer on the bedside table.

The room was warm and she threw off the sheet, arranging the pillows as a backrest, and poured out some
coffee. It was thick, black and sweet, pure ambrosia. She
sipped it slowly, her mind going over the strange night.

Dreams. Only dreams. She tried to convince herself
they didn't mean anything, but somehow it wasn't that
easy. She had always listened to the whispers of her subconscious, had always had an intuitive ability to size up
people and situations. Her father had said it was a gift
and not to treat it lightly.

Only with Jason had her instincts short-circuited. But now with the wisdom of hindsight, she realized this was probably because Jason hadn't let her into his inner self. He kept a mask over his emotions, showing little of the human being inside the astute businessman.

No wonder Sophie, used to the adulation of her father, had reacted like a hurt child to Jason's frequent indifference. Yet now she could feel shame at her immature behavior. She should have cultivated a deeper understanding of Jason rather than running away at the first excuse.

There was no excuse.

However, she thought, stirring restlessly in the comfortable bed, that was all water under the bridge now. Whatever it was that Jason wanted from her, she would listen to him, behave with dignity no matter what he suggested and then go on her way, back to her work and her ordered life. She had gotten over her infatuation with him, and despite her erotic dream, she was immune to his pull on her senses. She would not go back to being his wife; she didn't want a husband whose only interest was making money.

Later, showered and wearing a cool white sundress, Sophie went downstairs to the garden terrace where Stavros and Paul were seated at a glass-topped table set for lunch.

"Good morning," Sophie said wryly. "Although I suppose 'good afternoon' would be more accurate."

Paul jumped up and pulled out a chair for her. "Good morning, dear sister-in-law. The sleep has done you good." He spoke in Greek out of deference to his father as she had also done, although last evening she had learned that his English was as fluent as Jason's.

Stavros took her hand in his cool dry fingers. "Sophie, please stay with us for a while. You do look better than you did last night, but you are much too thin. You're all alone now, and you probably don't take care of yourself as you should."

Sophie was surprised at his apparent knowledge of her affairs. In last evening's conversation she hadn't mentioned her father's death, but it seemed they knew of it. "How did you know I'm alone now?" she asked curiously.

"News has a way of getting around," Paul said enigmatically.

Sophie would have pursued the subject, but Voula appeared just then with platters of salad and tiny fried fish. "Oh, look, my favorite," she exclaimed instead, with a smile of appreciation at the middle-aged woman who always treated her like a dearly loved daughter.

Jason hadn't shown up by dinnertime, and his brother suggested that he was unlikely to come home before tomorrow or the next day. They discussed mutual acquaintances during the meal, and inevitably Helen's name came up. Helen, the helpful, false friend who had contributed as much to the failure of Sophie's marriage as either Sophie or Jason; Helen, the snake in a designer dress who had used Sophie to stay near Jason while waiting for her chance at him, waiting, stalking, ready to pounce....

Had Jason been so unsuspecting?

With rigid control, Sophie asked if she still lived in Athens.

"She has an apartment here," Paul told her, "where she lives when she's not traveling about the jet-set watering holes of the world. Even though they were divorced, her husband left her the bulk of his fortune when he died. Don't you write to her, Sophie? I understood you'd been close friends.''

"We had a disagreement," Sophie said with masterful understatement, "and lost touch." She toyed with her fork, staring down at her plate, all appetite for the delicious *pastitso* suddenly gone. "Is she here now?"

"No, she thinks Athens is too hot in August. She went to New York a couple of weeks ago. Actually, she went with Jason when he was there on business, and she stayed on."

"Do you see much of her?" Sophie asked, delicately probing.

"She comes to dinner once in a while," Stavros said. "She's one of our few remaining relatives. I believe Jason sees something of her."

Sophie felt faintly ill. She picked up her water glass and drank from it to avoid making a further comment. Then Paul asked about a friend of the family who now lived in Vancouver, and the moment passed.

After they had finished eating, as soon as she decently could, Sophie pleaded jet lag and went upstairs, again to the master bedroom. Stavros' nurse, though unobtrusive during the day except for administering the old man's medicine, had not yet left, but Voula assured Sophie that tomorrow she would have the guest room.

This evening, however, sleep was determined to elude her. She lay wide-eyed and wakeful as memories of Jason and what had gone on between them in this room, and this bed, came back to ruthlessly plague her, like black bats released from a cave. In an effort to take her mind out of these dark caverns, she thought of her last meeting with Helen.

Helen, a distant cousin of Jason's and newly divorced at the time of Sophie's marriage, had taken Sophie under her wing and introduced her to Athens society. Sophie, away from home for the first time in her life, had embraced the sophisticated woman's friendship with eager innocence. Through her husband's business interests, Helen also knew Vancouver and some of the people Sophie knew. She visited the city several times a year, even after her divorce.

Some months after Sophie had left Athens to be with her ailing father, Helen had stopped by Sophie's house in Vancouver. She was dressed in mourning black due to the recent death of her ex-husband. Sophie had realized that despite their divorce, Helen hadn't been without feeling for the man whose main attraction she'd admitted was his wealth. Helen had nursed him through his final illness—not with her own hands, perhaps, but she had stayed at his side. Her devotion had been rewarded; her ex-husband had left her his millions and control of his international corporations. Helen was hardly a grieving widow, Sophie had seen at once. She'd worn an air of brittle triumph, and from the moment of her arrival she had treated Sophie with barely concealed condescension. Gone was the solicitous friendliness she'd shown in Athens.

Sophie had been bewildered and hurt by the change in the woman she had considered one of her closest friends, but not really surprised. Even in Athens, Helen had often made mildly malicious remarks about some of the people in their social circle—she didn't keep friends for long—and in her heart Sophie had known it would be only a matter of time before Helen would grow bored with her.

Then, too, Sophie had changed in the three months since leaving Greece. Nursing her father back to a measure of health after his serious illness coupled with the disillusionment of seeing her marriage disintegrate had matured her in a way even Helen had noticed at once. She had metamorphosed from a young, often foolish and impulsive girl into a woman who was beginning to understand her own feelings and goals.

At Sophie's father's invitation, Helen had stayed to dinner. During the meal she'd been pleasant enough, talking about Athens and about her husband's widespread business empire that she had been controlling—with the help of a large and competent staff of managers and accountants. She still had charm, Sophie had to admit, especially toward anyone of the opposite sex. Helen largely ignored Sophie, and the younger woman had listened quietly, wanting to ask about Jason without really understanding why. Jason hadn't contacted her since she had left; why should she care what he was doing?

After dinner, when Sophie's father had gone to his room, the women talked in a desultory fashion. Sophie soon wished Helen would leave. She was amazed that she had considered herself to have so much in common with Helen in Athens. Now they had nothing to talk about.

At last Helen rose and began gathering up her purse and gloves, preparing to leave. At the living-room door she turned to Sophie, a vindictive smile on her coldly beautiful face. "Haven't you wondered why Jason hasn't been in touch with you?" she asked, uncannily echoing Sophie's thoughts.

Warm color flooded Sophie's cheeks before she could control it. "Why, I—" she stammered, momentarily at a loss for words.

"He's been too busy with me," Helen stated, her gleeful eyes sparkling like ice chips. "You know," she added conversationally, "he only married you for your dowry, and now he no longer needs to keep up the pretense."

Sophie couldn't have been more astonished if Helen had dropped a real bomb rather than a verbal one.

"My dowry?" she repeated dazedly. "But Jason is a rich man."

"Now he is. The last six months have been phenomenally successful for him. Your father offered him a substantial marriage settlement, and he took it. It was only hard luck that he had to take you with it."

Sophie sank down into a chair. "How do you know this?" she asked weakly, despising herself for revealing what a blow this was to her.

"My husband did a good deal of business with Jason, and when he died I learned of Jason's past difficulties. It was fairly common knowledge among international financiers that many times in the last few years Jason was teetering on the edge of disaster. The worst time was when he married you. Your father's money bailed him out. Now with his spectacular luck, all his gambles have paid off, and he's a millionaire."

Sophie was stunned. Jason had never said he loved her, but his tenderness toward her, especially at the beginning of their marriage, and his unconcealed joy in their lovemaking, had been enough to calm any doubts she might have had—and she had to admit she hadn't had many. Now to come face-to-face with his mendacity, to find that he had cheated her and used her to further his passion for making money, shocked her to the depths of her being.

Helen was observing her closely with those eyes that looked like cold lake pebbles. "Surely you didn't think Jason actually loved you," she sneered, giving a harsh laugh that clashed with her polished appearance. "What a naive child you are!"

"Naive I may be," Sophied managed to retort. "But I wouldn't be so stupid again."

"Then why don't you give Jason a divorce, Sophie?" Helen said with no more emotion than she would use to discuss the weather.

Sophie went cold inside, as though a wintry wind had stolen all the heat from her blood. "What makes you think I won't?" she countered, her face absolutely colorless. She wrapped her arms around her stomach to stop its sudden heaving.

Helen shrugged, her shoulders lifting in a gracefully elegant movement. "He wants to marry me," she said, dropping her second bombshell. "If you give him a divorce, he can."

Speechlessly, Sophie had stared at the woman who was rapidly destroying all her illusions about loyalty and friendship. Then Helen dropped the final bomb. "We've been lovers since you left. In fact, Jason could hardly wait to get into my bed after you were gone. So you might as well set him free. You were never the woman for him anyway, Sophie. I grew up with him, and he's always felt responsible for me."

"But you didn't marry him?"

"No," Helen said quietly. "He was still poor, and I couldn't live that way. You've no idea how it was in that village—dirt floors, no bathrooms, sometimes even no water. I had to get free, so I married a rich man. I'll never be poor again. It was worth it to sleep with that old man, and he never knew how I hated it. I kept up my side of the bargain." Her face hardened into determination. "But now I want Jason."

Strangely, this deathblow had the opposite effect on Sophie. Far from demolishing her defenses, it caused her to reassemble a remnant of pride. She stood up, her face white but composed. "You may tell Jason that he can have a divorce any time he wants it. I won't fight it. But until now Jason has never asked me for a divorce. Perhaps he's not as anxious to be free as you would like to believe."

With a dignity beyond her years, she held the door open to allow Helen to leave the room. "And you may tell Jason also that I never want to see him again. Or you," she added coldly.

Her expression was so fierce that for a moment Helen looked nonplussed, but she made a rapid recovery, unable to resist a parting shot. "I'll send you an invitation to the wedding."

"Do that," said Sophie with icy calm. "But edge it in black. You won't be able to keep Jason any more than I could."

She'd gone up to bed in a stupor. To learn in one hour that both Jason and Helen had used her for their own ends was distressing enough; but to know that her own father had betrayed her and virtually sold her into marriage shook the foundations of her love for him. How could he have done it? The next day she intended to confront him with her knowledge. There had to be an explanation.

But subsequent events rocked her world even more severely, and the explanations did not materialize for months afterward. By then it hardly mattered.

A cold shiver went through her as she lay in the wide bed in Jason's room. Despite Helen's allegations that she and Jason were lovers, Jason had not contacted her about a divorce. The wedding invitation had never arrived.

Did he want a divorce now? Was that why he had lured her here, or was there some other, deeper reason?

With a sudden impulsiveness she decided that she would stay, at least until she found out.

Reluctant though she was to admit it even to herself, she was curious to see Jason again. Also, Stavros dearly wanted her to spend some time with him, and that was a compelling inducement for her to stay as well. She still missed her own father, although ten months had passed since his death. Stavros might have many years yet, but there was always the possibility that his heart would give out tomorrow—the angel of death didn't play favorites. Stavros had been a second father to her, had given his love to her with fewer ulterior motives than even her own father, and she owed him this small gift of happiness.

Besides, she hadn't had a real vacation since opening the shop. In the August doldrums, Laura could run it quite competently without her. She would relax for a few days, then perhaps scout the Athens clothing industry for items to send to Laura. It was time they added fresh lines to enhance their stock.

As for Jason, she could handle him. She didn't love him now, so he had no more power to hurt her. Let him do his worst, if he felt so inclined. The peace of mind and the strength of character she had so painfully attained in the past two years would see her through.

Two

Sophie must have slept at last, for it was the darkest hour of the night when the faint click of the doorlatch awoke her. Silhouetted against the faint glow of the night-light in the hall stood a dark and, to her sleep-fogged brain, menacing figure. She bit back a startled cry as she recognized, despite the passage of time, the arrogant stance of Jason, her husband.

He advanced into the room, closing the door decisively behind him, and switched on the bedside lamp. Sophie shrank back against the pillows, clutching the sheet up to her chin, her gray eyes wide and apprehensive.

He was much as she had last seen him, his expression guarded as he studied her. His black hair was perhaps a touch longer than he used to wear it, curling closely to his well-shaped head. Sophie had often thought fancifully that he ought to have had pointed ears like museum statues of Pan, but his face did not coincide with her image of the god of shepherds and pastures; it was too tough and hard, the chin too obstinate. His heavily lashed eyes moved over her in an unblinking sweep, their blue so dark as to appear black in the soft light, and she had the uncanny sensation that his gaze was penetrating the thin sheet and stripping her bare.

"Good evening, or rather, good morning, *yineka mou*." His voice was the same, deep and vibrant, his tone sardonic. The two intervening years vanished as an insubstantial mist. She heard again the same insolent inflection he had used in calling her a spoiled child, and she bristled, her eyes throwing angry sparks.

My wife, he called her now, but she no longer felt like his wife. He was a stranger; but for all her resolutions, she felt the aura of power that surrounded him, and, against her will, her senses stirred as some indefinable emotion passed through her. "Your father isn't sick," she said accusingly.

He didn't bother to deny the allegation as his mouth curved in a mocking smile. "So I misjudged the seriousness of his illness."

"You tricked me, and I'm leaving as soon as I can arrange a flight." In the heat of the moment, she forgot her decision to stay.

"You will leave when I say you may," Jason said in a silky voice that had an underlying steeliness.

"You can't keep me here," Sophie insisted with more confidence than she felt.

Jason was removing his jacket and tie. "We'll see." His hand went to the collar of his shirt, pulling at the knot of his tie. "By the way, Sophie," he said in a different tone, "I was sorry to hear about your father. I liked him."

"But not sorry enough to come to his funeral," Sophie retorted bitterly.

"It was a month later by the time I heard." He sounded sincerely regretful. "I was in the Middle East at the time, and you know what communications are like there."

She didn't, but she could imagine. He threw aside his tie and unbuttoned the top buttons of his shirt, then bent to remove his shoes and socks.

Sophie watched with dawning horror. "You can't stay here!"

One eyebrow quirked as another mocking smile fleetingly crossed his dark face. "Where would you suggest I sleep? This is my room and my bed. In case you've forgotten, this house has four bedrooms. My father is in one, the nurse in another, Paul in the third." He counted them out on his fingers with exaggerated patience as to a slightly dim-witted child. "And here we are in this one."

"Then I'll sleep on the living-room sofa." Sophie thrust back the sheet, preparing to step out of the bed, then subsided, remembering the thin material of her nightdress. Her robe was on a chair, but she could not reach it from the bed. A glance at Jason's derisive face showed that he was completely aware of her dilemma and would do nothing to alleviate her discomfort.

"Better if you stay here for what's left of the night." His tone was deceptively mild. He lay down on top of the sheet without taking off his shirt or the dark trousers. "I said sleep, Sophie. I'm tired, and all I want is to lie down and sleep." His lip curled contemptuously as she moved to the very edge of the bed away from him. "Don't worry, I've no designs on your body tonight." He turned on his side after switching off the light, leaving her staring at the broad expanse of his back.

The distinctive odor of his aftershave drifted to Sophie's nostrils, recalling the past even more vividly than actually seeing Jason. What is it? She had never smelled it on anyone else. Did he have it specially made for himself? Somehow she doubted that. Whatever his sins, vanity was not one of them. The scent must be merely the aftershave combined with the more subtle essence of his skin. All she knew was that his nearness still had the power to disturb her, no matter how she tried to deny it to herself.

Sunlight poured between the louvers of the shutters, laying strips of warmth across her face and waking her. For a moment she could not move; there was a heavy weight on her chest, constricting her breathing. Jason lay beside her, on his stomach, his outflung arm across her body. All the events of the night came rushing back, and she held her breath, fearing to wake him. When he did not stir, she edged carefully out from under his arm and fled in ignominious retreat to the bathroom, taking her clothes with her.

Jason was still asleep when she came out, the sound of the running water not having disturbed his deep slumber. He lay on his back now, one leg bent at an angle, the trouser leg creased and tangled, revealing a length of sun-browned calf that looked strangely vulnerable. His arms were flung high above his head, and the hard planes of his face were relaxed, softened by sleep almost to boyishness. Even now, with his animosity fresh in her mind, Sophie thought of how it had been for them

at the beginning and a feeling of sweetness surged
through her. She found it difficult to resist an urge to
smooth the tangled curls from his wide forehead, to drop
a kiss on his slightly parted mouth. Sternly, she hardened her resolve. After the way he had used her, he was
not deserving of any tenderness. She turned, stiff-
backed, and walked out of the room.

The table on the terrace hadn't yet been laid for
breakfast, so Sophie walked down the shallow steps into
the rose garden. Again, the day was fine, already hot in
spite of the early hour. She breathed deeply of the intoxicating scent of the roses and a border of stocks
nearby, thinking there was no place like Greece in the
summertime. Vancouver had a lush greenness, but the
weather was often rainy and changeable, as it had been
this summer. Here one had the feeling of endless summer as the sun blazed out of a cobalt-blue sky, day after
day with the same predictability as minutes turning into
hours.

She saw Voula placing baskets of rolls and plates on
the table and went to help carry out the silverware and
the cut-glass dishes of homemade preserves and *Hy-
mettus* honey, dark and thick as syrup, tasting delicately of thyme blossoms.

Paul was the first to appear for breakfast. He greeted
Sophie with a warm friendliness that lifted her spirits.
"You are looking exceptionally lovely this morning,
Sophie," he said, bringing color quickly to her cheeks.
He seemed to have shaken off the reserve with which he
had treated her on the previous day, and she realized that
it had probably been merely shyness, or perhaps deference to his father who had been present at all of their
earlier encounters. She knew that Greek children, even

long after they reached adulthood, usually behaved with utmost decorum in front of their elders.

"Thank you, Paul," she said, warming to the obvious appreciation in his eyes. She began buttering one of the fresh rolls Voula had brought out. Paul sat next to her, proving to be such a pleasant companion that it occurred to Sophie that, if Jason didn't prove too difficult, she could enjoy this visit.

Her equilibrium was shaken once again when her husband came out of the house, carrying his own plate and cutlery over the protests of Voula, who fluttered in his wake, scolding him gently. He answered with easy familiarity, his even white teeth showing in a good-humored grin. Voula, also from their village, had been working for them since Jason had improved the family fortunes, but she had known him since he was in diapers.

Jason seated himself opposite Sophie so that she was forced to look at him.

"Good morning, Sophie." Only someone who knew him intimately would have detected the underlying mockery in his soft voice. "You're up early. I trust you slept well."

Sophie rigidly schooled her features to betray no emotion as she politely assured him she had. Unbidden, the thought occurred to her that he had changed in one significant aspect that she had failed to notice in the dim light of the bedroom the night before. He no longer had the tense, driven look that had characterized him throughout the first year of their marriage.

Jason turned to Paul, asking him about the state of affairs at their local office. Then Stavros appeared, and under cover of Jason's greeting to his father, Paul whispered to Sophie, "Why didn't you tell me he was back?"

Sophie turned to him in surprise. "I didn't realize you wanted to know."

She glanced across at Jason, who was talking quietly with Stavros. He had changed his clothes, the dampness of his hair indicating he had showered. He must have risen soon after she had left the bedroom. His dark blue eyes suddenly swiveled to intercept hers, and she looked hurriedly down at her plate, but not before she had seen the expression that crossed his face. He seemed to be telling her without words: *I have something to say to you, but I can wait.*

As they were drinking their coffee at the end of the meal, Stavros asked Sophie, "What are your plans for the day? I expect you'll want to talk to Jason."

It was the last thing she wanted. "I thought I might go out and do some shopping," she said. "And perhaps go up to the Acropolis. That is, if you don't need me."

"No, it's your holiday. Do what you wish," he assured her, but he frowned as he said it. Was he thinking it strange that she would leave the house when Jason had so recently arrived?

Eagerly Paul leaned toward her. "I'll take you to town in my car." He glanced at Jason as he spoke, his expression half defiant.

Jason's black brows drew together. "Shouldn't you be going to your office, Paul? I understand you were home all day yesterday as well."

Paul flushed like a schoolboy caught with his finger in the cookie jar. "The business is going all right," he muttered sullenly.

"Nevertheless," Jason said levelly, "you'd better spend some time at the office, earn your salary. If Sophie wants to go anywhere, I will take her."

Sophie was dismayed. How could she wriggle out of being in Jason's company? She had originally planned to stay home and visit with Stavros; Jason's presence had been behind her sudden impulse to escape from the house.

"I can get the electric train to town," she said. "You needn't bother."

"It's no bother," Jason replied, unperturbed. "But it would be better if you stayed in today. I want to speak with you."

Sophie was silent, uncomfortably aware of the approval with which Stavros was regarding both of them. She hoped he would not be too disappointed when a reconciliation didn't materialize.

"Sophie," the old man said gently, seeing the mutinous set of her chin, "you'll have plenty of time for sightseeing. I missed you. You can't go out on your second day back."

Sophie knew she was defeated. She raised her eyes to meet Jason's hard stare across the table. "Yes, Sophie," he said softly, "we all missed you."

Not wishing to be drawn into an argument with him in front of his father, Sophie said nothing but gulped the last of her coffee, which had become cold and bitter, and excused herself. She almost ran into the house, stopping in the hall as Paul, who had followed her, called her name. "Sophie, if there's anything I can do—" he said, taking her hand in his.

Sophie shook her head. "There's nothing you can do. I can handle it."

His look was sympathetic. "Let me know if I can help. I'd like for us to be friends." He would have said more, but a peremptory voice behind him interrupted.

"Paul," Jason said harshly, "isn't it time you went to work? And would you please take your hand off my wife. Sophie belongs to me."

Paul dropped her hand as if it had suddenly burst into flames. "Excuse me," he muttered, and left. Sophie knew that for all his brave words he would be of little or no help against Jason. Jason had only to give his brother a hard look and he scurried like a frightened rabbit. Sophie was more nervous than ever, but she was careful not to let any emotion show on her face. In the two years on her own she had become expert at hiding her feelings, but now, with him looming over her, she could barely retain control and stand her ground. They glared at each other like two antagonists sizing each other up for a battle. Then mercifully Stavros came in and the tension snapped. He spoke to Jason, and Sophie was able to make her escape.

Upstairs Sophie looked through her handbag to check that she had enough money to get her into town. Once there, she could cash some of her travelers' checks. If she were quick she could get away while Jason was busy with Stavros.

She suddenly realized that the contents of her bag had been disturbed. In a panic she dumped all the items onto the neat bedspread. She was right—her passport was missing, and without it she could neither cash checks nor leave the country. Voula would never have touched her things; it had to be Jason. She remembered the soft way he had said "We'll see" the night before.

She sat on the edge of the bed, covering her face with trembling hands. He meant her to stay here and was going to some trouble to see to it that she did. Even if she went to the Canadian embassy and reported her passport lost, they would contact Jason. She knew some of the staff, but no one with the authority to issue travel documents without proper verification.

Her passport was in her married name, not for reasons of sentiment, but because her previous one had expired shortly after their marriage and she had applied for a new one using her new name. If she had known her marriage would be of such short duration, she would have retained her maiden name on this vital document.

What could she do now? She would have to appeal to Jason's better nature, if he possessed such a human quality, and she cringed at the thought of lowering her pride to beg him to release her. But after the way he had looked at her and spoken to her this morning, she was afraid he would not even listen to her appeals.

The door opened and the subject of her disquieting thoughts came into the room, closing it after him and leaning back against it. "Well, Sophie?" he said when she made no comment.

Cursing herself for being a coward, Sophie looked at him with tear-wet eyes. "Jason, let me go. Give me back my passport." She got up from the bed and stood facing him with as much bravado as she could muster.

Jason's eyes, often filled with mysterious shadows, now were as opaque as marbles and glittered coldly at her. "No, I want you here. We have some unfinished business, and I'll let you go when it's completed, not before. Besides, Stavros expects you to stay. You wouldn't want it on your conscience if he became ill at your abrupt departure. It bothered him a great deal when you left the last time, and his condition cannot withstand shocks."

Sophie wondered if this were true. She wouldn't put it past Jason to use Stavros' illness as emotional blackmail.

He spoke again, mildly, but with a coaxing note that caused her suspicions to mount. "Sophie, stay. Surely you're not scared of me. Stavros and Paul would instantly leap to your defense if I tried to hurt you. Besides, I hear it's been raining all summer in Vancouver, and we've had marvelous weather here. You're much too pale. You could use a little sun."

Jason asking instead of demanding? She almost laughed aloud. It had to be another trick, but that meant he was aware that she was no longer a green girl. As long as she understood his angle.... Her pride would never let her admit she was afraid of him, and she was just curious enough to want to see what his game really was. In any case, what he had said about the weather was woefully true.

"All right," she conceded reluctantly. "But only for Stavros' sake. And I have to have a room of my own. What about money? I have very little in cash, and I can't cash checks without my passport."

The triumph that gleamed in Jason's eyes caused her blood pressure to soar, making her wish she had never given in. His face softened fractionally as she glared at him, her cheeks flushed with impotent fury. He had won, so he could make concessions now. "I'll give you money for day-to-day expenses," he said. "The nurse is leaving—probably has already left—so you can have his room."

"Thank you," Sophie said stiffly. With her own sleeping quarters and his long working hours, she would be able to avoid him for the most part. The armor of reserve that had served her these past years would protect her at mealtimes and other occasions when she had to be in the same room with him. Perhaps when he saw that he could no longer influence her in any way, realized that she was indifferent to his charm, he would let her go.

Jason was still watching her narrowly, and she had an uneasy feeling that he could accurately guess the direction of her thoughts. The set look on his face reminded her of a leopard about to spring on its prey. She could almost see his tail lashing as he prepared himself for the kill, drawing it out as long as possible, enjoying the transfixed terror of his victim.

Sophie turned away abruptly. She must be becoming hysterical, she thought, fighting an insane desire to laugh. Jason was only a man, and there were laws to protect women from violence, even that of their husbands. Still, she couldn't forget that he came from a village in the Mani—that wild, remote area of southern Greece that had never been overtaken by any of the country's invaders, where families carried on blood feuds for generations, sniping at one another from the square towers that were the dominant features on the austere landscape.

Jason was suddenly so close behind her that she felt the heat of his body, even though he was not actually touching her. He moved like a leopard, too, his footsteps making no sound on the soft velvet carpet. Sophie shivered as he placed his hands at either side of her narrow waist.

"Sophie," he said softly, his breath warm against her nape, "I meant what I said downstairs. You belong to me." His hands began to move slowly upward. Their heat seemed to scorch her skin, even through her dress, and she drew her breath in sharply. At the small sound he stopped the movement, his fingers splayed across her body just below the curve of her breasts. Her heart fluttered like a trapped bird. She wanted desperately to move away from him, but her feet were rooted to the floor.

"I want you to stay, to be my wife again," Jason said, and she trembled at the possessiveness of his tone.

"You can't keep me against my will," Sophie said, her voice a thin, frightened thread of sound.

"Can't I?" he drawled sardonically, dropping his hands so suddenly that the places they had covered felt chilled. "Desperate times dictate desperate measures. Anyway, we'll see how long it's against your will."

Free of his touch, Sophie felt a surge of renewed courage. Her fright was rapidly being replaced by a hard, burning anger. "You barbarian," she stormed at him. "Why can't you behave in a civilized manner? What have I done to you that you think you can treat me this way?"

"Done to me?" Jason retorted, red color rising under the tanned darkness of his skin. "You left me." The way he said it was an accusation.

"You sent me away," she reminded him hotly. "You told me you couldn't stand the sight of me."

"I was angry. I didn't mean for you to go away for two years." His voice rose and Sophie cast an anxious glance at the door. Someone was going to hear them. "Two years!" he repeated vehemently.

He began to pace back and forth across the room. "Do you have any idea what it was like," he said savagely, "seeing people who knew us, having to tell them you had left me?"

He stopped in front of her and she shrank back, her legs coming up against the foot of the bed. His long fingers curled into fists at his sides, then uncurled, giving the illusion of a predator's claws. The flush had faded from his skin, leaving it ashen under his tan. He raised his hands as if to take hold of her, then as she flinched violently to the side, lowered them once more. He jerked away, resuming his pacing.

"I said your father was ill and needed you, but when you didn't return I knew people were saying you weren't coming back. You made a fool of me, Sophie. I can't forget or forgive that. And now you will pay. By staying here, for as long as I want you." He swung away and went out the door, slamming it so violently that a picture on the adjoining wall bounced, nearly falling before coming to rest askew on its hook.

Sophie stood for a long moment as the echoes faded, her burning eyes staring, seeing nothing. It would have been a relief to cry, but even this solace was denied her. He hated her. He had brought her here for revenge, and his words proved beyond all doubt that only his fierce Greek pride had been hurt by her departure.

She tried to pull herself together. She couldn't sulk in here all day. Her watch told her it was only half past nine. She was amazed. It seemed that a lifetime had passed since she'd gotten up this morning. She straightened her back determinedly. The first thing was to move her things out of this room with its memories that were beginning to haunt her. Now that the fatigue of the journey had worn off, she doubted she would be able to sleep in the bed where she had deluded herself that Jason loved her, once so long ago. She had hoped that the two years away from him had dulled the pain of disillusionment

and quenched the hot blood of passion that had en-
slaved her to Jason, but he had awakened with a few
harsh words all the forgotten torment.

She quickly turned her mind to the present. She must
at all costs avoid falling in love with Jason again. Thrust
into his company, she was not sure that she was strong
enough to resist him. He was a very attractive man, and
even knowing his faults she might again succumb to the
pull he had on her senses.

In the past, even after a vicious quarrel, Jason had
only to touch her with those magical hands and kiss her
with that seductive mouth for her to melt into his arms
with helpless desire. Helen's brutal words that winter
evening had shown her what a lie it had all been, how she
had let Jason weave a web of sensuality around her that
had blinded her into accepting an illusion of love for the
real thing.

With a grim little smile, she decided she would never
again be taken in by his deception.

Three

Sophie's repacking was accomplished in short order, and she went in search of Voula. She located her readily by following the sound of the vacuum cleaner, which Voula switched off immediately when she became aware of Sophie's presence in the neatly furnished bedroom just down the hall from Jason's. As the high-pitched whine subsided, Voula said, smiling at Sophie, "This will be your room. If you like, you can bring your things in now. I'm almost through."

With a thoughtful frown, Sophie went to fetch her case. Had Voula been in the room long? Its tidiness would indicate she had, and she had only been vacuuming for a few minutes. She must have heard them arguing—perhaps not Sophie's side, but Jason had not bothered to lower his voice. They had spoken in English, which Voula did not understand, but she would have heard the shouting and drawn her own conclusions.

Sophie set her case on the bed, carefully avoiding Voula's eyes, and began unpacking, hanging her dresses in the closet. Voula was flicking a dustcloth about the room. When she began dusting the dresser for the third time, Sophie could contain herself no longer.

"Well, Voula, what is it?" she asked brusquely, her voice sharper than she had intended.

Voula twisted the dustcloth in her hands. "It's none of my business—" she began.

"No, it isn't," Sophie said shortly. Then, seeing the embarrassed color that came into the other woman's face, she relented. Voula had always been a friend, almost a substitute for the mother she barely remembered. "I'm sorry, Voula," she said contritely. She laid her hand on the housekeeper's arm in a gesture of conciliation. "But Jason and I have to work things out for ourselves."

Voula put her arms around Sophie, the forgotten dustcloth still in her hand, filling Sophie's nostrils with the pungent smell of lemon-oil polish.

"Sophie," she said softly, gently, "if you could have seen Jason after he found you had gone, you would have come back, if only to save the rest of us from his wrath. He was beside himself. He gave up caring about his business, began drinking." Sophie was surprised. Jason rarely drank, never strong liquor, and only occasionally wine with meals. And to neglect his business! Voula had to be exaggerating. Yet she appeared perfectly serious as she continued, "Then one morning I found him unconscious on the living-room floor with an empty bottle beside him. I had to get the gardener to help me put him to bed. After that he stopped drinking. It seemed he never could remember the details of that night, where he'd been or how he got home, and it scared him.''

For a moment Sophie felt a twinge of guilt that she had so drastically disrupted Jason and the household, then she hardened her heart. He had also disrupted her, nearly ruined her life.

"Then why didn't he come for me?" she asked, freeing herself from Voula's arms.

Voula folded the dustcloth into a neat square, then into a precise triangle. "He's Greek, Sophie," she said at last, her voice serious. "He has pride."

"Pride!" Sophie snorted. "If he loved me he would have come to me."

"Maybe not." Voula shook her head sadly. "A man's pride is often stronger than his love. That's something we women have to face many times in our lives."

"He never loved me," Sophie stated positively. "He married me for the money my father offered for my dowry, and he expected me to be an amenable wife who would never make a protest about any of his activities."

"But you weren't so tame, were you?" Voula's face wore an amused smile. Then she sobered. "Sophie, you should have handled him differently. But you were so young. You've changed a lot. Get him to fall in love with you now. He has more time now, and it shouldn't be difficult."

"He hates me, Voula. I don't want someone who hates me. He'll always hold it against me that I injured his pride."

Voula regarded Sophie's stormy face with sympathy mixed with a degree of exasperation. "Don't be too impulsive, Sophie. I've known Jason since he was a boy, and his pride has on other occasions stood between him and a friend. I know," she added, going toward the door, "he's not the easiest of men, but don't forget he can be kind and generous." She went out, leaving Sophie to her unpacking and her thoughts that again were heavy with guilt. But exactly why, she wasn't sure.

At lunch only Stavros was at the table, reading a newspaper that he put down as soon as Sophie appeared. "Ah, my dear, I see you didn't go out after all." He smiled slightly, and she realized he undoubtedly was also aware of the argument she and Jason had had. Was nothing private in this house?

"No," she said stiffly. "I unpacked my clothes and pressed some of them."

His face lit up. "Does that mean you're going to stay for a while?"

"Yes, *Patera*, for a little while," Sophie told him with a measure of good grace. At least Stavros would treat her kindly, although she dared not go to him with all her anxieties. His heart condition would not be improved by worry or excitement, and she could not forget that despite the friendship between them, he was still Jason's father.

"Jason left here in his car, driving as if seven devils were on his tail, and he hasn't returned." Stavros' bright eyes took on a sly look. "Had he been speaking with you?"

"You are probably aware that we had an argument," Sophie said tartly, picking up her water glass and sipping from it.

Stavros feigned innocence. "Oh? Well, at least you're speaking to each other." He eyed her seriously. "Couldn't you make up with him? Jason needs you."

"Jason?" Sophie was incredulous. "I doubt that. Jason is a law unto himself and needs no one."

"Don't assume you know him yet," Stavros warned her. "You weren't married for very long, and the first year of marriage is usually not the time to build up a friendship. Passion gets in the way. I love my son, Sophie, and I know he missed you."

Crumbling her bread into her plate, Sophie was silent. From what Voula had said, she knew that Jason might have given an appearance of missing her, but she knew it was only because she had made him lose face.

The silence lengthened, and she had to come up with a reply. At last she said heavily, "I can't promise anything." She wanted to add that Jason didn't even like her now, much less love her, but she thought better of it. No matter what Stavros knew of their altercation this morning, her deep fondness for the old man would not allow her to state matters so bluntly.

She began to eat with little appetite, starting nervously as she heard footsteps along the terrace coming from the front of the house. She relaxed again when she saw it was only the gardener, having finished his lunch, going to the back garden.

"By the way," Stavros said pleasantly, fortunately having missed her agitation, "we have installed a swimming pool. If you'd like to use it, feel free to do so."

Sophie smiled. "What about you?"

"I'm sorry. These old bones can't take strenuous exercise any more. You're on your own." He winked at her mischievously. "Of course I'm not averse to watching.

If you want to swim after you have a rest, just follow that path. The pool is behind the hedge.''

After lunch Sophie went up to her room to lie down on the bed, which was equally as comfortable as the one in Jason's room. More so, in fact. This one was free of disturbing memories. She did not, however, fall asleep, and after an hour she gave up and changed into a swimsuit.

The house was silent as she slipped out into the heavy afternoon heat of the garden. The only sound was the constant monotonous hum of cicadas in the thick shrubbery that encircled the property, the unmistakable song of Greek summer. The roar of city traffic on the main road only a couple hundred meters away was so muted, she could almost imagine herself in the country.

Dropping her towel on a chair, Sophie stepped into the pool. The water was warm from the sun, blue-green and refreshing, sliding over her skin, soft as silk. Using an efficient crawl, she swam the length of the pool several times.

She turned over onto her back, only moving her legs enough to remain afloat, staring at the great blue bowl of sky above her, relaxing utterly and letting her thoughts drift at random.

She smiled as she thought of Stavros' always-easy acceptance of her. He never judged her, neither now nor during the year she had lived with Jason. And at that time she had done plenty of things to destroy his respect for her if not his affection. That idiotic spending of Jason's money on things she neither wanted nor needed. She knew now it hadn't been vindictive—it had only been a bid for Jason's attention, in the same way a child misbehaves to get his parents' attention. Had she really been that young, and that stupid?

Jason's accusations that she was a spoiled child, out of touch with reality, were not unjustified. Her father had protected her, kept her to himself as she was growing up. His money had provided her with the best schools, the best clothes, a lovely home, and had effectively insulated her from the full understanding that not everyone lived as they did.

As a teenager Sophie had rarely gone out with other young people. Her father had screened her friendships and the social events she attended. He had dominated her life and she, being a kindhearted, loving child, had not fully realized this, nor had she resented it. Perhaps that was why she had been shattered at the realization that Jason did not adore her as her father had.

The sound of a splash startled her. A dark head appeared beside her, and she straightened, treading water, laughing with relief when she saw it was only Paul and not Jason.

"Hi," he said nonchalantly, shaking water from his eyes like a wet seal. "So you didn't go out."

"No," Sophie said slowly. "I didn't. How was your day?"

He gestured carelessly with one hand. "The usual. I don't find managing a small branch office very challenging."

"Then why don't you ask Jason to give you more responsibility?"

"Do you think I haven't?" He grimaced, raking his hair back from his forehead. "But he doesn't think little brother is ready for the big time."

That morning Sophie had seen how Jason rode roughshod over his brother's feelings, although she couldn't help but think that in that particular instance he might have been justified. Still, Paul was hardly a child and Jason tended to treat him as if he were—and a rather simpleminded one at that.

"The way he practically scolded me at the table for not going to work this morning," Paul went on. "The office manages quite well without me. It's not every day I meet a beautiful sister-in-law."

"Wouldn't it be better if you applied yourself to your work, and proved that you're ready for more responsibility?" Sophie asked. "Even Jason wouldn't be so unreasonable." She was surprised to find herself defending her husband, but she knew that he would not tolerate inefficiency or slacking in others, least of all in his brother. Paul had had an easy youth, thanks to Jason, and someone had to take him in hand. She could sympathize with Jason's wish not to see his brother become an idle playboy.

Paul laughed wryly. "You don't know Jason as well as I do. He likes to lord it over the rest of us. It gives him a feeling of power to know that he paid for everything we have."

Sophie pulled herself out of the water and padded to the lounge chair where she had left her towel, her wet footprints drying instantly on the hot tiles. She raised the towel to dry the long pale strands of her hair. Paul swam back and forth for a time, then came out to flop down beside her, lounging on a cushion he had confiscated from a nearby chair.

"Did you get a job after you left Jason?" he asked idly.

Sophie smiled at his bent head. "In a way. I opened a fashion boutique with my friend Laura. I helped her with the financing, and she supplied the fashion know-how. It's worked out well."

Sophie certainly didn't need the money the shop brought in. Her father's estate, with his shrewd investments, would keep her in luxury for the rest of her life. But when Laura had approached her with the idea, her dream since high school, Sophie had enthusiastically gone into partnership with her friend. Now Laura handled the day-to-day running of the shop, while Sophie looked after the accounts, surprising herself with her good business sense and a love of the work.

"I'd like to check out the possibility of doing some buying while I'm here," she said to Paul now. "Especially hand-knitted items, which sell well in Vancouver."

"I'll give you a list of possible suppliers," Paul said, reclining on the cushion. His tanned legs were stretched out in front of him, and his green eyes were intent on her. Sophie realized that he had been looking at her for some time. She was suddenly self-conscious.

Shifting on the lounger, she looked about for her large beach towel. "I'd better go in. I'd like to shower before dinner."

As she sat up, she glanced toward the house whose chimneys were just visible above the surrounding hedge. Jason was standing in the open gateway that led to the pool area. Even at this distance of thirty meters or so, she could see the frown that drew his black brows together. She wondered how long he'd been there, watching what must have appeared an easy and intimate conversation between his wife and his personable brother.

Paul saw her expression and turned slowly to follow her gaze. As he did so, Jason turned abruptly, vanishing between the shoulders of the hedge. Paul made a sharp, profane exclamation. "Well, that does it. Now he'll think I've been playing up to you."

"Even he wouldn't jump to such a conclusion, would he?" But as she said the words, Sophie had a sinking feeling that that was exactly what Jason would think, especially if he were looking for something more to hold against her.

During the next several days, Sophie kept herself busy and out of Jason's territory, at least on an emotional level. Although he had taken her passport, he had left her credit cards. She was able to rent a car on her American Express card and made the rounds of the factories Paul suggested.

She put in a call to Laura. "So you haven't been lolling on the beach all day," Laura said with a bright laugh. "And how's the handsome Jason?"

Sophie made a face, which of course Laura couldn't see. "I haven't seen much of him, actually," she said with careful neutrality. "I'm sending a crate of clothes for the shop. Paul's arranging air freight, so it should arrive in the next few days, just in time for the fall displays."

"Good." But Laura seemed only marginally interested in the clothes. "Is he the younger brother? Maybe you should go after him." Her chuckle was unmistakable. "Or maybe I should come out there and give you a run for your money. It's been dead here."

Sophie laughed. "Never mind, it'll pick up. Bye, Laura."

"Bye, Sophie. Think of us sometimes, and don't forget to come back."

Sophie frowned as she put down the phone. How long could she stay? She still didn't know what Jason wanted. He hadn't mentioned the day he'd seen her with Paul at the pool. In fact, they rarely spoke at all. Only at times did the intense look in his eyes, meeting hers across a table or across a room, remind her of his presence. Yet his expression had ceased to hold anger, now holding a quality she couldn't readily identify but that was beginning to make her uneasy. He wanted something from her, but he was willing to wait and choose his own good time.

Sophie and Paul had become friends, developing a comfortable relationship that on her part was entirely that of a sister and brother. But sometimes she had an unsettling suspicion that Paul would have liked to show a deeper interest in her. She was careful not to encourage him, not only because she was tied to Jason, legally if not emotionally, but mainly because she did not want to be the instigator of more hard feelings between the brothers.

Paul had been diligently attending his work these days, but one day he came home unexpectedly for lunch. After the meal was over and Stavros had gone to his room for his usual nap, Paul persuaded Sophie, without too much trouble, to let him take her to the Acropolis. She did, however, stipulate that they be back well before the dinner hour. She was not consciously thinking of hiding the outing from Jason, but if he did not know of it she could avoid another confrontation with him.

Paul drove his car to the Kifissia terminal of the electric train, and from there they took the train to Monastiraki station. They walked across the site of the old

Roman market, with its impressively restored Stoa of Attalus, toward the entrance of the Acropolis hill. Sophie closed her eyes for an emotional moment, remembering the sense of homecoming she had had on that first day back in Athens. From the taxi she had seen the Parthenon floating in a golden mist of sunset, serenely removed from the traffic snarling on the streets below, traffic that was hastening its ultimate ruin.

A guide approached as they made their way up the wooden steps under the Propylaea, but Paul waved the man away with a few brief words in Greek. The fierce sun blazing from a hard blue sky turned the marble underfoot, worn smooth as glass by the passage of unnumbered thousands of feet, to molten silver with a brilliance that hurt the eyes.

Sophie would have been content to spend the entire afternoon puttering about the ancient monuments, but after an hour Paul was restless and bored. Sophie was surprised at his attitude, which she considered unseemly in a native-born Greek. Jason had always enjoyed taking her to his country's many archaeological sites—when he had the time—proud of Greece's varied and often turbulent history.

"Let's go down and have a coffee at the Grande Bretagne before we go home," Paul suggested with a trace of petulance in his voice.

"You go if you want," Sophie said absently, gazing up at the Porch of the Maidens. "I can find my own way home."

"I want you to come with me," Paul insisted. "I don't want to drink coffee alone."

"All right," Sophie said impatiently, making a mental note not to let Paul take her to any more ruins.

They had almost reached the row of taxis in the parking lot when a strong voice called Paul's name.

"Damn!" he muttered. "How did he know we were here?"

Jason strode toward them, anger darkening his face, grim purpose showing in every line of his lean, supple body. Ignoring Sophie, he addressed himself to Paul. "Jake Anderson telephoned from New York about the computer contract you were working on. When he couldn't reach you at home, your secretary called my office. Voula told me she thought you had come here."

"Is he going to call back?" Paul asked, a dark flush staining his cheekbones.

"Yes, at five-thirty," Jason said grimly. "If you get one of those taxis, you should be able to reach your office in time."

Paul hurried away and Sophie was left in the unenviable position of being alone with her glowering husband. When he spoke his tone was mild enough, his face shuttered, but she had an impression that beneath that facade he was smoldering. "Do you want to look around any more, Sophie? Perhaps visit the Agora? I know Paul is bored very quickly with history."

Sophie had wanted to, but the arrival of Jason and the ensuing unpleasantness had taken away her appetite for sightseeing. "I'd rather go home. It's awfully hot, and my feet hurt."

The smoldering rage in Jason burst into flame. His hand shot out and, heedless of the curious glances of passersby, he gripped her upper arm with painfully hard fingers. "Do they?" he asked tightly, his eyes flashing blue sparks. "Or is my company so repugnant that you'd rather skip one of your favorite pastimes than have me accompany you?''

He dropped her arm and began to walk quickly toward his car without looking back to see if she was following. For one crazy moment, Sophie debated taking a taxi; then she discarded the idea as childish. Besides, it would put off the inevitable, making the explosion all the greater when it finally occurred.

The concentration needed to navigate through the heavy traffic left little room for anger. Jason glanced at Sophie as she dejectedly, stared out the side window. Damn it, why did he have to behave like a clumsy schoolboy around her? How could he approach her and make her understand that he didn't hate her?

Abruptly he steered the car off the main road in the direction of Mount Penteli. If the peace and grandeur of his secret place didn't move her, nothing would.

Sophie clung to the armrest as Jason sent the Jaguar racing up the narrow road. He braked slightly as they caught up to a truck whose undercarriage sagged beneath the weight of an enormous block of marble, then swiftly overtook the laboring vehicle. After a moment Jason turned off the road onto an almost overgrown track that seemed to lead to nowhere. Long grass and small bushes scraped against the bottom of the car, that and the deep purr of the engine being the only sounds in the oppressive silence and breathless heat.

Jason brought the car to a halt outside a heavily padlocked gate in a high stone wall surrounding what was evidently one of those small churches scattered throughout Greece used only on special feast days. He got out of the car and, coming around to Sophie's side, opened the door for her to get out. Still without a word, he took her arm and led her around the outside of the wall to a small group of stunted pine trees. Their sharp, resinous scent filled the hot air as the slight breeze blowing on this unprotected height sighed softly through the upper branches, rustling the summer-dry needles.

"What is this place?" Sophie asked nervously.

They had come to the edge of the pine grove where the mountain formed a rampart, falling away abruptly at their feet, displaying a vast panorama of purple-gray hills covered with low shrubs, their sparse leaves burned by the relentless sun that was now lowering, gilding the far summits of Mount Parnes.

"This place?" Jason responded at last, his anger seemingly gone. "Just a church. I come here sometimes to be alone when I'm tired of the city. All this—" he gestured toward the mountains spreading in awesome loneliness away from them "—reminds me of the village where I was born. The countryside there is just as big and empty."

He fell silent, his face bleak and withdrawn, lost in his thoughts, none of them pleasant to judge by the frown that furrowed his brow. Sophie stood gazing at the scenery, so near the city yet so utterly silent that they might have been on another planet. Loneliness and sorrow tore at her heart, making her want to cry, but gradually peace came to her.

Without a word Jason took her hand in his and led her back to the car.

"I want you to leave Paul alone," he said suddenly, shattering the harmony that for a moment had existed between them. "He's not attending to his work the way he should, and his absence from the office today may cost us a valuable contract.''

"I didn't know," Sophie said softly. "I thought he had the afternoon free."

Jason glanced at her sharply. "You like Paul, don't you?"

"Yes, I do." Sophie spoke almost defiantly, an intonation Jason was quick to pick up.

"You're still my wife, Sophie," he said in a low, dangerous voice. "And don't forget it."

"I'm not likely to, am I?" Sophie said resentfully. "You've made me your prisoner as well."

Jason did not bother to refute this. "All prisoners should have as luxurious a prison," he said dryly. "You haven't been denied anything, have you?"

"Only my freedom," Sophie retorted furiously. "Jason, let me go back to my own life. What's the point of keeping me here?"

"Point?" he echoed hotly. "You're my wife. You belong with me."

"I haven't been a wife to you for two years. Can't you accept that I don't want to be your wife anymore?"

The look in Jason's eyes as they slowly moved down her body told her as plainly as words what he was thinking. She shivered in spite of the oppressive heat. She knew that in his imagination he had stripped her naked. "I could easily make you my wife again," he said silkily. He paused for the briefest second, then added even more softly, "But not yet."

Sophie itched to strike the knowing, almost leering smile off his face. "You Greeks think you know everything about women. You're all far too arrogant for your own good."

His brows rose. "We Greeks? Have you forgotten you're as Greek as any of us?"

"My mother was English," Sophie reminded him stonily.

"Yes, and probably that's what contributed to your flightiness."

Sophie made no reply to this unsubstantiated and unjustified remark, and after a moment Jason spoke again. "Come, we'll go home. This isn't getting us anywhere."

In the garage at the house he turned to her again before she could leave the car. "Just remember, Sophie, leave Paul alone. I could make things very unpleasant for you."

"What do I tell him?" Sophie flashed. "That his big brother says hands off? He has never put his hands on me."

Jason's eyes turned black. "And he'd better not try," he muttered savagely. Then he seemed to control his temper. "Just try not to be alone with him. Paul is an impressionable boy, and he gets bored with his toys quickly."

Sophie's simmering anger boiled over. "Is that how you think of me? As a toy?" She choked and was forced to swallow hard before she could continue, her voice controlled but bitter. "But that is all I ever was to you, isn't it? You never saw me as a real person." She broke off again and flung open the car door. "It's useless to even talk to you." She slammed the door shut and ran toward the house, tears blinding her eyes.

Four

At the end of the garden grew an enormous old fig tree whose branches touched the ground, forming a cool green cave around the trunk. During the few months she had lived in this house prior to the breakup of the marriage, Sophie had often come to this haven when she wanted to be alone, and she thought of it as her special place.

It was here that she came in the breathless heat of midafternoon on the day following the ill-fated trip to the Acropolis. She had seen neither Paul nor Jason, both of them evidently having left for their offices before she had come down for breakfast. She'd been purposely late in order to avoid them.

She wondered if Jason had said anything to Paul, warning him off. Despite Paul's softness of character, which was in marked contrast to Jason's toughness, she knew that he could be stubborn, too, once he set his mind on a thing. Any warning of Jason's might well have the effect of spurring him on to greater overtures toward Sophie. She had not imagined the antagonism and rivalry between the brothers, and would not put it past Paul to use her to score against Jason.

Sophie had no wish to cause an irreparable rift between them, but she liked Paul, and he could be a good friend. Yet the danger was not only Jason's possessiveness, but also the fact that no Greek male would be content for long to have a platonic friendship with a woman. She was protected for the moment by her marriage, but if Paul gained the impression that their marriage was truly over, he might decide to put pressure on her for a closer relationship.

Sophie lay back in the softly fragrant dry grass that carpeted the ground under the tree, trying to shut out her disturbing thoughts. Sunlight filtering through the abundant green foliage made a pattern of light and shadow that dappled her dress and bare limbs, overlaying them with leopard spots. She stretched her legs, relaxed like a cat in sunshine, absorbing the peace and quiet. She could hear bees droning lazily among the flower borders, and near her hand an ant struggled to drag a leaf to its nest, passing with difficulty over a stone rather than taking the easier route around the obstacle. Single-minded determination—if only one could be an ant or a bee, without the problems that beset humans, with only one purpose in life: to store food for the winter, to survive.

She was on the verge of sleep when the curtain of leaves parted and Pan entered the glade of the forest nymph, shattering the peace as explosively as a crystal goblet smashes on a marble floor.

Sophie's eyes flew open, their gray depths clouded and bemused. Jason sank down beside her, his dark, handsome face unsmiling and closed. His white shirt was open, revealing the thick black mat of his chest hair, and his tanned, muscular legs were bare below snug-fitting shorts. He must have left his office early if he were already home and changed into casual clothes.

"What are you doing here?" stammered Sophie, disconcerted by the intense look he was giving her. She sat up, pulling her dress down to cover her knees.

Fixing her gaze on Jason's chest, mere centimeters away, she studied the pattern of hair covering his golden brown skin. She was uncomfortably aware of his nearness, of his scent compounded of warm skin and aftershave and cleanliness. She wanted to move away but was afraid to—afraid of his derision if she showed fear. Her eyes wandered lower as if they had a will of their own, past his trim waist, skipping over the tight shorts that did little to conceal the masculinity of him, down to his long legs.

Jason seemed blissfully unaware that he was not welcome. "This is where you used to come, too, isn't it? I must keep it in mind. It's peaceful here."

Sophie said nothing, vowing never to come here again. She had thought of it as her private refuge, and now he was taking even this from her. She moved as if to rise, but he sensed her intention and took hold of her wrist, not tightly but with enough pressure so that she could not free herself without a humiliating struggle. She remained still, watching the ant's laborious progress with the leaf.

Jason followed the line of her gaze. "I'll bet you never had time to relax in Vancouver, did you? Sophie, why are you so anxious to get back there? If you stay here I'll take care of you, and you'll have time to yourself and to enjoy sunsets and lazy afternoons."

Puzzled by his apparent good nature when she had expected him to continue where he'd left off yesterday, Sophie looked into his face. His dark blue eyes were narrowly studying her, the heavy lashes masking their expression.

"What about when winter comes?" she asked.

His shoulders lifted in an enigmatic and very Greek shrug. "Let tomorrow bring what it will." His voice changed, became softer, persuasive, so that alarm bells began to clang in Sophie's head. "Sophie, I want you to stay. You could open a shop here if you wanted. Come and live with me again. It would mean a lot to Stavros."

"And to you?" Sophie could not stop herself from asking.

He averted his eyes. "To me, too," he muttered. "I missed you, Sophie, whether you believe it or not."

"Only in your bed," she retorted sharply.

He looked at her and his eyes darkened, but whether with remembered passion or with anger she could not tell. "Admit it, Sophie, we had no problems in that area, did we?"

"But you hardly spoke to me outside of that," Sophie said bitterly, "except about inconsequential matters."

"It could be different now, if we could try again."

"Does the leopard change his spots?" Sophie said sarcastically. "You were brought up to think of women in a certain way, and you'll never change."

"As you wish." He shrugged again, an indolent gesture that irritated her. "But Stavros would be very happy to see grandchildren. He's not getting any younger."

Alarmed, Sophie's eyes flew to Jason's face, but he was looking at the ground and appeared unaware of the change in her at his words. She said quickly, to cover her sudden agitation, "Then perhaps you should divorce me and marry again so that you can give him a grandchild." She was pleased that she kept her voice steady, giving no inkling of how her heart was racing.

Jason sat up straight. "You are my wife. My children will be conceived with you," he said harshly. "Or not at all."

Sophie was frightened by the implacability in his tone. "Not willingly," she snapped.

"You were always more than willing, as I recall." His smile was wolfish.

There was a short, pregnant silence, then he went on. "Don't expect me to believe there has been no one in these two years," he drawled sarcastically. "From what I know of your sexual appetite, you wouldn't have survived without a man for this long."

Sophie was appalled. Jason, who had always delighted in her eager and uninhibited response to his lovemaking, now made it sound as if he thought her nothing more than a cheap tart. Something curled up and died inside her, leaving her cold as ice, but when her instinct was to crawl away and give vent to the awful tears flooding her soul, pride came to her rescue.

Summoning a taut little smile she said sweetly, "You'll never know, will you, Jason? And some of them may have been better lovers than you."

She knew she had struck home as his eyes blazed with ungoverned rage and jealousy. She had a fleeting impression of another emotion crossing his face, but it was gone so quickly she decided she must have imagined it. He couldn't have been hurt.

His mouth set in a cruel line that frightened her so that she almost cried out, but who was there to help her? Before she realized what was happening, he leaned forward and pushed her onto the grass-cushioned ground. One of his long legs swung over to trap both of hers, pinning them to the ground so that she could not move, his thigh abrasive against her smooth skin. His head came down toward her until she could see all the little sun lines radiating from the corners of his eyes. Then his face blurred as his mouth fastened on hers in a cruel, punishing kiss that drove the breath from her body.

As the first shock wore off, Sophie lay unmoving, staring with wide-open eyes at the green canopy of leaves over her head, some corner of her mind registering the sweetly ecstatic warbling of a wild canary in the treetop. Jason, after the initial hardness of his mouth, was not hurting her although his weight lay heavily on her. His kisses now were gentle and persuasive. She recognized his skill, but for the first time since meeting him he left her completely unmoved. She felt nothing—nothing at all.

For a moment she was fiercely glad—he could no longer dominate her with his potent sensuality. Then she became alarmed. Perhaps she would never again be able to experience that rush of hot blood, that delicious, breathless anticipation that finally culminated in an explosion through her body until all her nerve endings were bathed in a golden glow.

Desperately she tried to bring up some memory of past lovemaking. Still she felt nothing. He was kissing her throat and the hollow behind her ear, his mouth warm and insistent, and she lay there, limp and unmoving. She tried to tell herself that it was really Jason, whom she had once loved, who had once been her husband, but it didn't seem real.

This is Jason, her mind cried—Jason who had once brought her alive with only the slumberous look in his eyes. But her body wasn't listening. He was kissing her with devastating expertise, and she felt as if she had died and would never come alive again.

"Agapi mou," Jason murmured.

Sophie snapped out of her lethargy, the heat of anger suddenly burning away the chill of her body. She struggled against his hands and, taking him by surprise, succeeded in freeing herself sufficiently to sit up. "I'm not your love," she snapped furiously.

"No," he agreed, the inscrutable mask once more in place over his dark face. "Not anymore."

Sophie was brought up short. What did that mean? Had it been love he had once felt for her? No, she thought wearily, if he had loved her he would never have let her stay away for two years. It was the money from her father that had driven him to marry her. The fact that she was a beautiful woman might have appealed to him for esthetic reasons, but was hardly a basis for deep emotion.

"Why did you marry me, Jason?" she asked with bitter weariness. "Was it just the money my father gave you? He always said he wanted me to have a husband who could support me. You were capable of that."

Jason sat up abruptly. "How did you know about the money?"

Had he thought it was a secret? "Helen told me after I left here. And my father confirmed it. Later he was sorry he'd done it, when things turned out the way they did."

"I want you for my wife," Jason said roughly. "Do you understand?" In a quieter tone he added, "The money no longer matters. I paid it back not long before his death."

"How? I didn't see your name in any of his business records when I went over them."

"It was through our lawyers."

Sophie was conscious of relief at this piece of news. As long as she thought her father had traded her to Jason for the money, she had carried a burden of resentment that had not been dissipated by his explanation that he'd done it for her own good, to protect her from fortune hunters. Good for whom, she had asked him bitterly at the time. And wasn't Jason only a slight cut above a fortune hunter?

"If that's the case," she said, "it releases me from any obligation to you."

"Didn't your wedding vows mean anything to you, Sophie?" Jason asked with a curiously dispirited droop to his mouth.

"Of course they did," Sophie said with feeling. "I kept them. You broke yours."

"Did I?" He looked at her strangely, searchingly, then moved close to her once more. Before she could react he had his arm about her shoulders and was kissing her again, with lingering intensity.

When he raised his head, she glared at him. How dare he use kisses and caresses merely to prove his superiority over her? "I hate you," she whispered venomously.

"Good," he said. "That's better than indifference."

To Sophie's surprise, Jason made no further attempts in the next few days to kiss her, and he did not seek her out when he knew her to be alone. He was unfailingly polite to her at mealtimes, drawing her into conversation and being generally the perfect host. She could not help wondering what game he was playing.

One day Paul, apparently disregarding Jason's warnings as she had feared he would do sooner or later, came home early. Sophie's first intimation of his presence came when she heard a splash at the opposite end of the pool from where she was floating, giving her an odd sensation of *déjà vu* until she recalled that he had come upon her in the same way a week or two earlier. She swam to the edge of the pool and pulled herself out, reaching for her towel. Paul came to stand beside her, in water to his waist.

"Good afternoon, Sophie," he said rather grandly, deviltry dancing in his green eyes.

"Aren't you supposed to be working?" Sophie asked.

"Everything is under control," he told her cheerfully. "There wasn't much going on, so I came home. It's awfully hot in town today."

"Did you get the contract the other day?"

"Yes, we did, so Jason got over it. He did warn me off you, though," he added, an irrepressible grin showing his excellent white teeth. "But while the cat's away—" His voice trailed off significantly.

Sophie was hard put not to laugh at his jovial expression, but she set her mouth primly in what she hoped was a severe look. "Don't behave foolishly, Paul. Jason could make a lot of trouble for you."

He laughed carelessly. "I can handle it. Besides, I like you and I like being with you." He laid his hand on her knee. "Don't you like me?"

Sophie gently removed his hand. "I like you, Paul, but as a brother. I am Jason's wife."

"He doesn't treat you like a wife," Paul asserted, all humor gone from his face. "You don't even share a room. If you were my wife, I wouldn't leave you alone every night."

Sophie pulled her legs under her and arose to her feet. "I'm sorry, Paul, but it's between Jason and me. We have to work out our differences ourselves."

Paul also climbed out of the pool, water streaming from his body. Sophie noted with clinical detachment that he was lighter about the chest and shoulders than Jason, less muscular. He was deeply tanned and looked very fit and strong despite his slighter build.

Taking a towel from a nearby table, he slung it about his neck, raking his hair back from his forehead with the other hand. "Sophie, how long are you staying?"

She paused in the act of rubbing her long hair dry with the thick towel. "Why, are you trying to get rid of me?" she asked flippantly. Then seeing he had no answering smile, she sobered. "I don't know, Paul. Jason has my passport, and he won't let me go."

"The hell!" he blurted explosively. "That's barbaric."

Sophie shrugged. "Maybe, but what can I do? I don't want to upset your father, so I can't ask him for help, or even advice. Besides, he thinks a woman's place is with her husband, and may consider that Jason is within his rights."

"I suppose he would," Paul agreed, his brow creasing in a thoughtful frown. "I wonder what game he's playing. He can't just keep you prisoner."

Sophie smiled ruefully. "Try telling that to Jason."

Paul's eyes ranged over her as she stood in her brief swimsuit. In spite of her fair hair, she tanned quickly and was already a pale gold. "He hasn't harmed you in any way, has he?"

"Of course not," she hastened to assure him. "In fact, he usually ignores me except when your father is around."

"Do you want to leave?" Paul asked, watching her keenly.

Sophie had a feeling she knew what was going through his mind. Something about the psychological phenomenon of the hostage falling in love with the kidnapper. She shook her head. "No, it's not what you're thinking. Any feelings between us are dead. I just want to leave, to get on with my life." But did she really, deep down inside, she wondered with a confusion she was careful to hide.

They began to walk toward the house. "Do you think it would do any good if I spoke to him?" Paul asked.

Sophie stopped short. "Paul, please don't. He would be very angry if he knew I told you this at all. Please don't speak to him. He'll get tired eventually and let me go."

"All right," Paul said reluctantly. "But I still think it's wrong. I knew he was possessive, but this is going a bit too far."

Sophie saw the stubborn look that was beginning to come into his face, an she was absurdly reminded of Jason at his most implacable. "Paul," she pleaded, "promise me you won't say anything to Jason. At times he scares me."

Paul patted her arm absently, deep in thought. "Okay," he said at last. "I won't, but come to me if you really get into difficulties. I'll try to help."

"Thank you, Paul. I won't forget this."

"Good girl." Paul grinned. "I think I'll go back and have another swim. All this serious discussion has made me sweat again." He strode away from her in the direction of the pool.

In the house Sophie found Eleni, the daily maid, in the main bathroom washing the floor. In spite of her cooling swim, she felt hot and sticky. The day was airless and humid, most unusual for Athens; but perhaps a storm was brewing. She went into her room for a robe, deciding to shower in Jason's bath. He was not due home for another hour, by which time she would be through and back safely in her own room.

She let the cool water course over her in a soothing stream, lathering her hair generously with sweet-smelling shampoo. Her spirits, which had been sinking lower and lower in the last few days, were slightly more buoyant now after the talk with Paul. At least she had an ally—of sorts. Although if it came to the crunch, she did not think Paul would stand a chance against Jason's forcefulness.

She turned off the water and opened the shower door. Her arm froze in the act of reaching for the towel as she saw Jason leaning against the edge of the washbasin. For a moment she was too stunned to cover herself. His dark blue eyes swept over her, missing nothing. He was fully dressed in a lightweight suit, making her all the more conscious of her nakedness.

She found her voice after what seemed an eternity. "Get out of here," she spat viciously.

"Why should I?" His tone was insolent in the extreme, though she could detect no trace of emotion on his dark features. "It's my bathroom."

"Eleni was cleaning the other one," Sophie stated. "How did you get in here? I locked the door."

"That lock hasn't worked in months." His keen eyes had not left her for a moment. "Besides, it's not as if I've never seen you. We used to share everything."

Against her will, heat suffused her body as she remembered that at the beginning of their marriage they had shared everything, often even showering together. She snatched the towel and wrapped herself in its voluminous folds.

"You forfeited the right to share things with me," she said hotly.

"You left me," he reminded her remorselessly. "I didn't drive you away, no matter what I said in anger."

"Oh, didn't you?" she queried sarcastically, her fine brows lifting. "By your conduct, you did."

Jason spread his hands in a peculiar gesture, almost of helplessness. "I don't know why you thought what you did, but it was all in your imagination. We could have talked it out."

"Don't give me that, Jason," Sophie retorted rudely. "You never had time to talk to me, and when I tried you got on your high horse and walked out. It was all over Athens that you were unfaithful."

Jason shrugged. "Believe what you like. Nothing I can say will convince you." He straightened from his indolent stance, drawing up to his full height. "However, I think the time has come for you to be a proper wife again. We'll start by moving your things back into this bedroom. You will sleep with me, in my bed."

Sophie's mouth opened and closed, but no words came out. Was he psychic, aware of Paul's statement "he doesn't treat you like a wife"? "Jason," she finally managed to get out on a strangled note, "I can't."

"You can and you will. I wouldn't want Paul to get any more ideas about our relationship." He went toward the door and Sophie could not see his face.

With his hand on the door handle, he paused and half turned toward her. Sophie still stood in the middle of the floor, the towel clutched around her, water dripping down her legs and forming a puddle at her feet. "To set your maidenly fears at rest, remember I said *sleep* with me. That's all for the moment." Humor briefly lit the darkness of his eyes. "Though I imagine it won't be long before you want more than that." He flipped up his immaculate cuff to reveal his watch. "You have forty-five minutes before dinner. That should be ample time to move your things."

Another fleeting smile crinkled the corners of his eyes, and Sophie fumed inwardly that he could find her dismay so amusing. "Oh, and close your mouth. A bird might fly in." Whistling airily he went out, closing the door softly behind him.

Sophie snapped her mouth shut, her blood boiling at his audacity. She began to rub her legs vigorously with the towel. She would show him. She would be as cold and unresponsive as a marble statue. She didn't think for a moment that he would keep his word and not make love to her. It would be easy to foil him. The other day in the garden had proved she was immune to his lovemaking.

He would soon tire of her, being the virile man that he was, and would lose no time in sending her packing.

Then why did she suddenly feel so bleak at the prospect of leaving?

Five

In the Stephanou household, dinner was usually taken early by Athens standards; many people did not eat the evening meal until eleven or later. This evening, instead of being filled with a pink and gold sunset, the dining room was gloomy from clouds gathering in the western sky.

The air was close in spite of the open windows, and Sophie felt stifled. The unease of her thoughts increased the foreboding in her, the black clouds seeming to be portents of evil, symbols of Jason's anger that would fall on her head when he discovered she had not complied with his instructions.

Neither Paul nor Stravros appeared to notice any atmosphere in the room other than that of the threatening storm, although Paul cast her several questioning looks as she merely picked at her food without eating any of it.

The intermittent growling of thunder in the distance suddenly erupted in a resounding crash that had them all jumping out of their seats. The delicate lace curtains billowed into the room, and Jason leaped up to close the long windows. A rain squall whipped across the terrace, driving before it bits of leaves and broken twigs, heavy drops beating a tattoo on the window glass as Jason forced it closed in the teeth of the increasing wind. Lightning crackled viciously, and the thunder that immediately followed was the sound of all the chariots of heaven storming across the sky.

Water streamed down the windows as the black clouds dumped their accumulated load. In Athens it seldom rained in summer, but when it did, it was with the force of a dam bursting. Lightning flashed blue in the room, its magnesium brightness eclipsing the light of the overhead chandelier. The lamp flickered and almost went out as the bolt must have struck some vital electrical fitting.

Then, as quickly as it had begun, the rain ceased with the suddenness of a tap turning off, the thunder receded to an indistinct, bad-tempered mutter, and the last rays of the dying sun glowed redly in the room.

They had spoken little during the awesome display of the forces of nature, but now the clatter of plates and cutlery being washed in the kitchen seemed unnaturally loud. Jason gestured to Sophie to accompany him out to the terrace, and with visible reluctance, she did so. Paul made as if to follow, but his father spoke to him.

"Paul, stay here. There is something I want to talk with you about." Looking anything but pleased, Paul subsided in his chair.

Outside, the terrace floor was rapidly drying, the tiles still retaining the heat of the afternoon sun. The air was clear as a bell, fresh with the scent of wet earth and growing plants. Whoever figures out a way to bottle the fragrance will make a fortune, Sophie thought, breathing deeply.

The terrace continued around the house, and Jason led Sophie, with a light hold on her upper arm, out of sight of the dining-room windows.

In the eastern sky hung a perfect rainbow, the colors pink and mauve and green, brilliant as a child's paints against the angry purple-black clouds.

Sophie drew in her breath in wonder. "It's beautiful," she whispered.

"I thought there would be a rainbow," Jason said complacently, as though he had stage-managed the whole thing himself. "That's why I brought you out. Not for the nefarious reasons you were so quick to suspect of me."

She looked sharply at him. So he remembered the delight she had always taken in nature and the outdoors. Somehow this did not tie in with the insensitivity with which he often treated her. Could it be that he was softening toward her, even regretting his dictate of the afternoon? Then she grew cold as the thought came to her that this might be only another event in his campaign to bring her to her knees, give her a kindness with one hand and twist the knife with the other.

"Thank you," she said coolly, concealing all her thoughts behind a composed, polite-guest face.

The air was chilly now that the sun had gone, and she hugged her arms around her body. A blue twilight hung over the garden, softening the outlines of the plants, giving them a misty dreamlike appearance. *L'heure bleue*, a snatch of remembered French drifted through her head. In a few minutes it would be completely dark.

Jason did not appear to notice the chill, even though he wore only a thin silk shirt. He stood leaning on the wall that surrounded the terrace, staring broodingly over the garden.

Sophie turned toward the house. "I'm cold. Are you coming in, too?" The awe she had felt at the sight of the rainbow had dissipated, leaving her sad and empty.

"Sophie, what have you been saying to Paul?" Jason spoke without turning.

Sophie's heart jumped into her throat. "To Paul?" she echoed. "Why, nothing. I've hardly seen Paul." She added bitterly, "You saw to that."

Jason came toward her, his features unreadable in the gloom. "I thought he looked at you strangely during dinner."

"You must be imagining things," Sophie said coldly. "I'm going in."

Jason moved swiftly and reached her before she came to the corner of the house. His long fingers clasped her upper arms, only firmly enough to keep her there. "Sophie, I know you haven't moved your things." The words came tightly through clenched teeth, as though he was having difficulty controlling his temper. Then his tone softened. "Please, Sophie, I'd like us to have a proper marriage again. How can we in separate bedrooms?"

Sophie was not going to be fooled by his change of tactics from force to coaxing. Anger still lay beneath the quiet words. "Take your hands off me," she hissed an-

grily, mindful of Stavros and Paul in the house. "I can't
bear for you to touch me."

The venom in her voice must have penetrated, for he
let go and she stalked into the house. She paused before
entering to smooth her hair unnecessarily with a shaking hand and to compose her face. Jason had not
followed.

In her room later, after a shower, Sophie sat at her
dressing table smoothing cream on her face. She was
wearing a white lawn nightdress, the least transparent
one she owned. She was undecided as to her next move.

If she went to bed in Jason's room he would assume
she had capitulated without further argument, and this
was an impression she wished to avoid giving at all cost.
On the other hand, she was afraid of what he would do
if he found she was not in his room.

He would not dare make a noisy scene with Stavros
only a few steps down the hall. Or would he?

With one ear open for any sound from the hall, Sophie wiped the excess cream from her face, discarding
the tissue in the wastebasket. She heard nothing—Jason must still be working in his study.

Halfway between the dressing table and the bed, she
hesitated. Should she go to bed and hope that if he found
her asleep he would not disturb her? The hour was not
late, and she didn't feel the least bit sleepy. Besides, the
tension of waiting for the storm of Jason's anger would
keep her awake.

Pulling on a light robe, she curled up in an armchair
with a book. Let him come—they would settle it once
and for all.

When Jason finally came she was sleeping in the chair, her long, pale hair half covering her face. Jason stood watching her for a moment, his face inscrutable. Then he gently touched her shoulder.

"Mm," she muttered indistinctly, snuggling further into the chair. Then, as awareness that this was hardly a comfortable bed came to her, she sat up.

"Jason, what are you doing in my room? Has something happened to Stavros?" Her mind hazy with sleep, she had forgotten their quarrel.

"You were supposed to be in my room. Since you weren't, I came to you," he said evenly.

Before she could protest he drew her from the chair, stripped off her robe and swung her up into his arms. She had a fleeting impression of a warm, bare chest before he put her down on the bed, and her breath caught in her throat. Was he naked? Licking her suddenly dry lips, she looked at him. No, he wore silk pajama trousers that, though thin, observed the proprieties.

The mattress sank slightly as he lay down and pulled the single sheet up to cover both of them. "Good night, Sophie," he murmured, bending over and kissing her with a light, tender touch of his warm mouth.

He rolled away before she could react and pointedly turned his back, leaving her fuming at how neatly he had tricked her, and plotting improbable and mainly unworkable methods of revenge until tiredness and overwrought nerves took their toll, and she slept.

She was in a dark wood, the trees naked as in winter, their leafless boughs poking holes in a heavily clouded sky. Wind sighed eerily through the bare twigs, clattering them together until they sounded like hysterical voices mock-

ing her. She was filled with a nameless fear and foreboding. How had she got here? Where was the house?

Suddenly, at a distance she heard the faint cry of a child, a thin and hopeless wailing on the wind. She began to run toward it, running, running, until her breath rasped in her throat, but the sound seemed to come no closer.

A twig cracked and she looked back over her shoulder. A dark and menacing figure, illuminated for an instant by the fitful moonlight, was following her, clad in a hooded cloak. The moon brightened again, and she saw that the figure had no face, only a black nothingness under the hood. She cried out in stark terror and ran faster as the cries of the child sounded nearer. She gave a ragged sob, scarcely able to catch her breath. She had to save the child.

Faster—faster—I can't—I—can't—

The wind increased until it was howling, the sound of women mourning the death of an only son. Bare branches clutched at her like chill, grasping fingers, holding her back, slowing her down.

The ghastly pursuer was almost upon her. She stumbled on an exposed root, falling to her knees. Something pulled at her clothes, and she could not move. She shrieked into the wind, twisting out of reach of the powerful horror who was preventing her from going to her child.

Whom could she call for help? Jason? She would call Jason. No, she realized hopelessly, not Jason. Jason hated her, and he was far away.

But there was no one else. She screamed with renewed panic as the dark figure was upon her, bearing her to the ground. "No, let me go. Jason! Save my baby."

She looked full into the faceless hood and a shaft of moonlight fell on it, revealing the face. It was Jason. She screamed again and fell into a black oblivion.

Sophie awoke covered in a cold sweat, her frantic heartbeat choking her as if she really had been running. Her face was pressed against a warm, furry surface that moved gently up and down. She was sobbing, on the verge of hysteria. A soft voice murmured words that meant nothing to her, only the sound was infinitely soothing, spelling warmth and security.

Gradually her crying lessened, and she became aware that she was being tightly held in Jason's arms. For a moment, disoriented and still frightened, she struggled against the steely strength of his embrace, then sensing it was futile, that she could not escape and did not really want to, she rested against him.

Gradually she worked her mind back to reality, and comprehension of her position returned. She pushed herself abruptly away from contact with him.

Jason let her go at once and, reaching out one long arm, snapped on the bedside lamp. Sophie lay back against the pillows, her face pale and distraught.

"You had a nightmare," Jason stated unnecessarily.

Sophie closed her eyes wearily. "Yes," she whispered. "I've had them before."

Jason grasped her shoulder with hard, demanding fingers. "What was it about, Sophie? Tell me." His voice was harsh. Then he shuddered. "The way you were screaming, like a soul in torment."

Sophie shook her head, her hair spread on the pillow, silvery as captive moonbeams in the lamplight. "It's always the same—someone chasing me. I've had it many times, but not recently. I thought it had gone away." She sounded tired and hopeless.

"When did it start?" His hand was hurting her so that she could not prevent herself from crying out. "Sorry," he muttered, loosening his grip. "Did it start after you left me? I would have remembered if you'd had them before. You always slept like a baby."

Sophie opened her eyes and met his. "Yes," she said, knowing it was useless to evade his questions. "It started a few months after I left."

Jason's eyes gleamed triumphantly. "So it did bother you to leave me. I thought you weren't affected at all."

The nightmare had started only after the other traumatic event in her life, which she must never let him discover, but it was simpler to let him go on thinking the obvious. "Yes, it did affect me," she flared. "But I'd do it again. I had to leave you. I couldn't stand the way we were living."

For a moment they glared at each other in silent enmity, the air crackling with tension. Jason broke the deadlock by turning off the lamp and lying down on his side of the bed.

There was an almost tangible tension between them still, and Sophie knew that Jason was as wakeful as she was herself. After what seemed a long time she grew drowsy and was on the edge of sleep when his voice came to her again.

"Sophie, you cried out, 'save my baby.' What baby?" The words were spoken without particular emphasis, but she had a feeling he was intensely interested in her answer.

She was glad of the darkness lest her face gave her away. "I don't know," she said, her heart racing. "In the dream I heard a baby crying. That must have been it."

The quality of his silence was more eloquent than any comment would have been, but he said nothing more and after a moment turned on his side away from her.

Sophie awoke to bright sunlight slanting into the room from the window where the shutters stood partly open. Jason, obviously having just got up, was crossing the room to the door. With sleepy eyes she watched him. Wearing only the thin pajama trousers, he was the very image of masculine virility. Even after yesterday's arguments and her resentment toward him, Sophie couldn't help admiring the sheer male beauty of him.

"I didn't know you'd taken to wearing pajamas," she taunted him, driven by a perverse imp of provocation.

He refused to rise to the bait, replying coolly, "I've probably changed in other ways as well." He went out, closing the door.

Sophie, disappointed at his mild reaction, rolled over onto her stomach. Only the dent in the pillow and a couple of stray black hairs on its snowy surface remained to tell her that Jason had really slept there. That and the faint aroma that lingered on the sheets.

The smell brought back vivid memories of the first months of their marriage when she had been so happy with no clouds on the horizon. Everything had seemed to take on brighter colors, richer tastes, and intensely pleasing odors. He had brought out a sensuousness in her nature that she had never suspected she possessed. Strange, she mused sleepily, how scents recall past events and people to the mind. She had loved the smell of Jason's skin; that, more than any other aspect of him, was a powerful aphrodisiac. She knew she was not unique in this feeling. Psychologists had discovered that a woman could not fall in love with a man whose particular odor was disagreeable to her.

How warm and comforting his arms had been in the night. A secretive smile touched her lips, then as remembrance struck her, she sat bolt upright, the smile turning into a gasp of dismay.

The nightmare. She had had the nightmare again, and now Jason knew about it. Did he suspect anything, that it was more than just a dream? Perhaps not yet, but when he had had time to consider, his sharp mind would undoubtedly draw its own conclusions. She hoped it would not be too soon. She must arm herself to be casual and continue to pretend that nothing had disturbed her life other than the failure of their marriage and later the death of her father.

The others had long since gone, and Stavros was on his last cup of coffee when Sophie arrived at the breakfast table.

"Good morning, my dear," Stavros greeted her with a twinkle in his blue eyes. "Did you sleep well?"

"Yes, thank you," Sophie answered, hiding her slight annoyance. Somehow or other Stavros knew that Jason had slept with her and, being Greek, had come to the obvious conclusion. There was nothing she could do or say to deny his notion of a happy reconciliation without hurting him.

She spread butter on a slice of toast and bit into it. She was aware of Stavros' bright eyes on her and wondered what was on his mind. She hadn't long to wait.

"Sophie, Jason mentioned that he would like to give a small dinner party for a few friends next week. I think it's a good idea, don't you? Everyone will be happy you're home."

Dismay brought a bright flush to Sophie's cheeks, and she hurriedly averted her face from Stavros. Another nail in her coffin, she thought ghoulishly. Why had she ever come? She must learn to control these softhearted impulses. The cords of the net were closing around her, and there was nothing she could do to escape their clinging bonds. Habit ingrained from childhood and her own kind heart had entangled her more surely than any coercion from Jason.

Stavros was waiting for her comment, and she mustered her pride, smiling a brittle little smile that fortunately fooled him. "That would be nice, *Patera*," she said, but in her heart she thought venomously: *Jason, I'll kill you when I see you again*. How could he increase the invidiousness of her position by involving his own father? Had he no scruples whatever? She realized with certainty that where his pride was concerned, he had none.

Six

Sophie managed to wait until after dinner that evening before giving vent to her feelings, which were in a fine fettle after having smoldered all day. She had kept a polite front, though with difficulty, during the meal, and by now she was ready to explode. Since there was not much point in making a further issue about the rooms—obviously Jason could sleep with her any time he wished, with or without her consent—she had decided to relent and move to the master bedroom, where the confrontation took place. Her clothes were already installed in the closet as though they had never left—Voula's work, no doubt, on Jason's orders, and this added fuel to the fire of her grievances. Everyone aided and abetted Jason. No one even thought to consult Sophie's opinion in matters that so directly concerned her.

"What are you trying to do?" she blazed at him as soon as the door closed. Her flashing eyes in her highly colored face gave her a beauty of which she was completely unaware but that did not pass unnoticed by the man before her.

"What's ruffled your feathers now, Sophie?" Jason queried in a mild tone that incensed her further.

"You know what! The dinner party. You want to show me off as if everything is all right."

Jason appeared singularly unmoved by her impassioned words. "I thought it was about time we invited some people over. It's common knowledge by now that you're living here, and people are probably wondering what's going on since we don't go out or invite anyone to our home." He stepped forward and touched his fingers to her obstinately set chin. They lingered for an instant, then trailed slowly down the pure line of her throat. She took a step back, hating him with her stormy gray eyes.

"People will think I torture you," Jason went on, unperturbed.

"Do you really care what people say about you?" Sophie demanded.

He shrugged in that irritating manner. "Not particularly, but too much talk would be bad for business. Some of the people I deal with have a very traditional attitude toward home and family."

This only confirmed what she had suspected: that it had been politic for Jason to acquire an attractive and amenable wife. Her dowry had been a factor; but if she had been a different type, she knew he would never have contemplated as final a step as marriage. He would have raised the money by some other means.

But the last two years had taught her to stand on her own feet, to realize her own worth. She wasn't the same person he had married, the shy, compliant virgin, the sheltered Greek girl who let first her father and then her husband determine her destiny.

"I won't do it," she announced defiantly. "I won't come down for the dinner, pretending everything is all right. I'll stay in my room."

"Our room," Jason corrected, with set teeth. He put his hands on her shoulders, bringing his face close to hers, willing her with all the force of his personality to meet his eyes. "You will come down," he said in a dangerously silky voice, "even if I have to drag you. And don't think of doing something to disgrace me. Your own pride won't let you. You know it as well as I do. So you will behave as my wife and act as though you're enjoying it."

"I won't," she retorted childishly. "And you can't make me."

Jason's eyes glittered ominously. "You underestimate me, my dear. Once I could make you do anything. I think it will still work. Like this." His mouth clamped down hard on hers with a brutal force that stopped her breath, grinding her lips against her teeth, which she stubbornly kept tightly clenched. He raised his head for an instant. "Or have you forgotten?" he added mockingly.

This time his kiss was softer, seductive, as he used all his skill and expertise to arouse her. It might have been the comfort he had given her in the night, or the result of her anger, but this time she was unable to remain indifferent. Against her will a once-familiar sensation came to life in the pit of her stomach, its heat spreading downward with the inevitability of an incoming tide. With stubborn determination she held herself rigid in his arms. She would rather die than have him suspect she was anything but cold and unmoved.

She gasped, almost giving herself away, as he gathered her closer, one hand moving slowly down her back to her hips, drawing her firmly against him. She was instantly aware of how aroused he was, and a long-dormant desire began to flame in her. Desperately trying to stop her insane urge to melt into him, she kept her mouth closed and her eyes open as his lips trailed hot fire down her creamy throat. She began mentally counting from a hundred backward, giving the operation all the concentration she could muster.

Jason straightened, relaxing his hold slightly, and looked searchingly into her pale face. His eyes were glazed with passion, a look she remembered well but had never thought to witness again.

Sophie swallowed hard in an effort to moisten her dry mouth. "May I go and get ready for bed now?" She kept her voice carefully steady and devoid of emotion. "I'd like to take a bath." She added with scathing contempt, "It doesn't work anymore, Jason. I felt nothing. Do you hear me? Nothing!" Her voice rose shrilly on the last word and almost broke. "I can't stand your touch," she choked. "It makes me feel dirty."

This time she had gone too far. She saw the savage look that leaped into his face and wished with all her heart that she could retract the words. "You used to beg for my touch," he spat out.

Fury made her even more reckless as she scattered all caution to the winds. "Before I knew any different.

Maybe you're not the great lover you thought you were," she taunted.

His face terrible, contorted with rage, he swung his hand back. Sophie braced herself for the blow, horrified now yet too proud to cringe; but it never landed. Instead he took hold of the two edges of her shirt and ripped it from her, the buttons flying in all directions. His face was white with fury, and a thick blue vein pulsed at his temple, looking as though it would burst any second. The plastic fastening at the front of her bra snapped easily under his fingers, and he threw the lacy garment across the room.

Picking her up bodily, he strode to the bed and dropped her on it, where she lay too stunned to defend herself, the breath knocked out of her.

"Now," he said, pulling off his own shirt, "we'll see how cold you really are, and what kind of a lover I am."

He threw himself on the bed next to her, one leg holding down both of hers. His face was still angry but under control as he lowered his head toward her. Instead of the harshness she expected and that she had braced herself to endure, his kiss was soft, his mouth moving over hers with warmth and tenderness, a tenderness designed to arouse her.

The tip of his tongue came out and traced a path around her lips. Still she would not open her mouth to allow him entry, although the fear in her was rapidly being devoured by a blaze of desire such as she had never expected to experience again.

She must not give in to him. She was her own woman, not a chattel of Jason's, available for his convenience. If she fell under his spell again, she would never be free.

She had to stop him, but how could she while he kissed her with such devastating sensuality?

When his mouth moved down her throat she could talk again, but the dangerous excitement increased, weakening her limbs and her resolve. Jason lifted his head for a moment, his eyes hot and desperate.

"Sophie, please," he groaned in anguish. "I need you so. Please let me have you."

And unknowingly, he gave her the one weapon she could use to retain her sanity. He thought she was still unwilling. Unless she said yes now, he would stop. Jason was not a man who would take a woman to bed by force; he had too much pride.

She moaned under the onslaught of his mouth when it engulfed her nipple with liquid fire, struggling to retain the last shreds of reason. Pulling at his thick black hair, she cried desperately, "Stop, Jason. You wouldn't take me unwillingly." And only she knew she lied.

For a moment she thought she had failed, that he was too far out of control to hear her. Then, abruptly, he thrust her from him, moving to lie on his stomach beside her, his breathing harsh and ragged in the silent room. Sophie lay on her back, aching for herself and the ungratified need in her but, strangely, more for Jason. All the anger seemed to have been driven out of her, leaving only an abyss of sorrow.

Unnoticed tears ran slowly down her cheeks until one in her ear forced her to acknowledge that she was crying. Crying for what might have been? Or crying for a hope of a future for them without a tug-of-war over who was the strongest? She didn't know.

After what seemed an age, Jason got up from the bed and, without so much as a glance at her, went into the bathroom. Presently, when she heard the shower running, Sophie arose, stripping off the remainder of her clothes. She put on her cotton robe.

When Jason came back into the bedroom, his face was pale under his tan but without expression. His eyes, black with indefinable shadows, flicked over her briefly, and she met his gaze unflinchingly. If he saw the traces of tears on her cheeks, he made no comment. Lifting her head proudly, she got up from her chair and went past him into the bathroom.

Sophie ran a hot bath and lay in it, thinking it would relax her. Her thoughts were not conducive to relaxation, however, and even the heady scent of the bath oil did not give her pleasure.

Why had she been so sure that it would cause irreparable damage to their relationship if she had given in to Jason? Why had she been concerned about his feelings at all, about his pride? Could it be that her emotions were not as dead as she had wished them?

With self-contempt she admitted that she had wanted him to make love to her, and the wanting had not been purely physical. She had wanted him since that disastrous episode under the fig tree. Her lack of response then had been an illusion.

At the thought of his long hands caressing her, she felt flushed with a heat that owed nothing to the bath water. He still excited her, but in a wholly different way than he had at the beginning of their marriage. Then, she had let him make love to her, let him give pleasure to her body without much thought of his feelings. Now she was concerned with his needs, not only physical but emotional as well.

What had brought about this change in her? She had grown increasingly restless in his presence in the last few days but had ignored what should have been warning signals. She was not indifferent to him at all, and Jason certainly wasn't indifferent to her. He might hate her, but he desired her.

Sexual love had always been wonderful between them. Even when other areas of their relationship had deteriorated, they had still had this uncontrollable physical attraction. Only in the last month together had their lovemaking become sporadic as their quarrels had become more vicious, reinforcing Sophie's doubts about Jason's faithfulness.

But was physical attraction enough of a foundation on which to build a marriage? She was certain it was not. But could it be a start? Jason seemed more willing to listen to her than he had two years ago, and he was certainly less of a workaholic than he had been. Since the explosive chemistry between them was still very much alive, perhaps it was just possible to work out an equitable solution.

She sat up abruptly, causing a tidal wave that nearly overflowed the bath. What was she thinking? Go back to Jason? Beg to be hurt again?

An undeniable truth impinged on her consciousness. She loved Jason—probably had never stopped loving him. How could she have been so blind that she hadn't seen it before this? It had been lying in her subconscious all this time. She had no longer wanted to love him and had managed to override her emotions with logic and suppression of her natural instincts.

She almost groaned aloud in dismay. She couldn't love him—she had to conquer this weakness in herself. Love made one vulnerable, susceptible to hurt, and she had vowed the last time never to let Jason hurt her again.

She stood up and reached for a towel, her mind racing. If she searched deep in her soul, was the prospect of being his wife really so unthinkable? Could she seduce him into loving her and so create a relationship that would insure her happiness? Or would this increase his contempt for her?

If she loved him, she would want him back on any terms. That was what all the romantic novels said. But real life was not so simple. She had matured and knew she would not be able to live with a man who had no respect for her, no matter how much she loved him.

After putting on her nightdress, she brushed her teeth and crept silently into bed beside Jason. She had barely settled when he shifted over next to her. She jerked away from him, her heart pounding. Was he about to carry on where he had left off?

Jason stiffened, then said gently, "Sophie, don't. Please don't. I'm not going to touch you. I hate myself enough as it is, without hurting you more."

She was silent, too surprised at the pain and the pleading in his low voice to think of anything to say.

Jason reached out a hand to her, then pulled it back. "Sophie, I'm sorry. It was unforgivable."

She had to say something. Tears thickened her voice. "I'm sorry, too. I shouldn't have said what I did." Suddenly, she couldn't let her pride stand between them. "I lied about the other men," she mumbled, wanting to hide her face in his chest and cry and cry.

The room was too dark for her to see his face, but even through her tears she saw the way his eyes glittered as he jackknifed to a sitting position. "Is that true, Sophie?"

he asked in a strange voice husky with an emotion she could not begin to analyze.

She swallowed her tears. "Yes," she said. She turned her back, lying on the very edge of the mattress.

"Why, Sophie?" he said insistently.

He did not touch her or cajole her in any way, yet some force emanating from him compelled her to answer.

"I didn't want a lover. I'd had enough of men, living with you." She didn't care if she sounded rude. She had to keep a distance between them. If he touched her now, she would go up in flames.

Jason lay down again. "And now you don't even want me." He sounded curiously defeated. There was a long silence, then he added softly, "But maybe we can change that."

Sophie spent a restless and boring day, unable to settle into any activity. She still had the rented car and had thought to take Stavros for a drive down to Sounion, but he was out visiting a bedridden friend.

She was no nearer to a solution to her problems than she'd been last night. Jason seemed gentler, more inclined to be considerate of her thoughts and feelings, but could she trust this change in him? Did she even dare to? Happiness for her seemed at an impossible distance. The best solution would probably be to go back to Vancouver. If Jason really cared, he would come after her. Yet this decision was not easy to make, either. Last night had kindled a tiny hope that their marriage might yet be salvaged, and on terms she could live with.

He had never apologized before....

In the late afternoon, unable to bear the confinement of the house a moment longer without going mad, she

Silhouette Desire are love stories that go *beyond* other romances — taking you behind closed doors, to share the intense, intimate moments between a man and a woman united by love.

These are fascinating stories of successful modern women, who are in charge of their lives and career — and in charge of their hearts. Confident women who face the challenge of today's world and its obstacles to attain their dreams and their desires.

At last an opportunity for you to become a regular reader of Silhouette Desire. You can enjoy 6 superb new titles every month from Silhouette Reader Service with a whole range of special benefits: a free monthly Newsletter packed with recipes, competitions, exclusive book offers and a monthly guide to the stars, plus extra bargain offers and big cash savings.

As a special introduction we will send you Four specially selected Silhouette Desire Romances when you complete and return this card.

At the same time, because we believe that you will be so thrilled with these novels we will reserve a subscription to Silhouette Reader Service for you. Every month you will receive 6 of the very latest novels by leading Romantic Fiction authors, delivered direct to your door. And they cost the same as they would in the shops — postage and packing is always completely Free. There is no obligation or commitment — you can cancel your subscription at any time.

It's so easy. Send no money now — you don't even need a stamp. Just fill in and detach this card and send it off today.

decided to go for a walk. The relentless Greek summer was softening toward autumn. It was still hot, but in the pleasant, tree-lined streets, the heat was bearable.

Sophie's thoughts dogged her footsteps, making her heedless of distance or direction. Walking along the almost deserted street, she clenched her fists until her nails dug into her palms. Why didn't Jason ever let her see his inner self? Only in the dark did he ever talk to her. Only in the dark was he ever gentle, only in sleep vulnerable.

Why did he always hide?

The sun was low in the sky when she realized what a long way she was from home. She had come without a purse and didn't even have money for a taxi. She could take one and ask the man to wait at the house while she got the money, but if Jason was home, as he was highly likely to be at this hour, she couldn't bear to see his derision.

Darkness had fallen when she finally trudged up the walk, limping painfully from a blister on her heel. All her fears were realized as Jason himself opened the door before she had a chance to knock. She had also forgotten her key. Obviously he had been looking for her, and it was equally obvious that the long wait had done nothing to improve his temper.

"So you've finally decided to come home." His voice was heavy with sarcasm, but she saw in the bright hall light that his face was strained. Alarm sharpened her tired brain. Had Stavros had another seizure? His next words belied this notion, and she sagged with relief, letting his anger wash over her without taking it in for a moment.

"It's not safe for a woman to walk alone here after dark," he raged.

She could not ignore his shouting and retorted, "Compared to Vancouver, Athens is as safe as the inside of a house. Besides, why should you worry? If something happened to me, you'd be free." *And so would I,* she thought dismally.

A strange expression flitted across his face, gone too quickly for her to interpret. His midnight-blue eyes studied her with unnerving intentness. "That depends on your idea of freedom," he muttered oddly. He paused for a second, seeming to gather his thoughts from somewhere. Then he said quietly, "Sophie, don't do it again."

"I will if I please," she said defiantly, tired and disheveled, and chagrined that he should see her at a disadvantage. "How will you stop me? Put an armed guard around the house?"

Jason grasped her by the shoulders. "Promise me you won't do it again," he implored her earnestly, all anger gone. "Athens isn't the way it used to be." He pulled her against him, his hands stroking her sweat-dampened hair back from her brow. "Sophie, promise me."

Alarmed by the sudden quickening of her heartbeat at his nearness, Sophie freed herself, muttering, "All right. Now let me go and wash for dinner."

She managed to walk steadily up the stairs, but she was conscious that his eyes never left her until she turned at the landing.

In the bathroom she examined her foot. The blister had broken, leaving an ugly red sore. She bathed it carefully, wincing as the disinfectant stung the wound, then applied a strip bandage. She put on backless sandals, arriving at the dinner table just as Jason was sitting down.

"Where's Paul?" she asked in surprise.

"He was invited out to dinner," Jason told her briefly.

They ate in virtual silence, Sophie wondering if he would go to his study after the meal as he usually did. He didn't. He carried the coffee tray into the living room, signaling Sophie to pour out the coffee.

The dinner and a glass of wine mellowed him. He shook off his reserve, asking Sophie serious questions about her business and news of people he knew in Vancouver. Sophie relaxed as the tension between them seemed to recede for a time.

Later, when he said he had some work to complete in the study, she went up to prepare for bed in a happier frame of mind than she had been in all day.

She must have slept before he came up. She was only aware that sometime in the night she turned, half awake, and felt his reassuring presence beside her in the bed.

In the morning she awoke in a sun-filled room to find Jason up, clad in his bathrobe, his black hair still damp from the shower. With complete lack of embarrassment he removed the robe and began dressing. At the sight of his lean, naked body, desire clutched at Sophie's insides, and her fists clenched under the covers with the force of it. All the passionate feelings she thought she had conquered came back in a fiery rush. The sensation she had experienced the other day was nothing compared with the fire that threatened to consume her now.

As he was buttoning his shirt, his eyes met hers in the mirror. "Good morning, Sophie." The words were a deliberate caress. How much had her expressive face given away?

She could not answer; the words seemed stuck in her throat. If he noticed her pink cheeks, he gave no further sign but went coolly on with his dressing and finished by snapping the catch of his slim gold wristwatch.

"I'll see you tonight," he said evenly. "Have a good day."

Not quite sure what devil drove her, Sophie got out of bed. With a deliberately seductive sway, she advanced toward him, aware that the sun shining in the window turned her nightdress into cobweb transparency.

The coolness deserted Jason's face. His eyes glittered with the desire that sprang hotly into them. "You too, Jason," Sophie said, brushing her lips over his.

Before he could react, she ducked into the bathroom. A moment later the door closed with a slam that seemed to epitomize frustration.

Sophie leaned her forehead on the cool, tiled wall and groaned with the acuity of her own desire, her nails digging into her palms.

What idiot had said "revenge is sweet"? Obviously someone who'd never loved.

Saturday came and Sophie went down early to help Voula with preparations for the dinner party. She had decided that she couldn't in all decency defy Jason in this matter. He had made tentative moves toward her, ambiguous though some of them might be, and she was willing to reciprocate to the same extent. She would show him that she could organize a meal he wouldn't be ashamed to serve to the elite of the city. She would rather that the tightly knit business community of Athens talked about the success of her party than have them criticize her. She hadn't forgotten their quarrel about the dinner, but her own pride, as Jason had so accurately suggested, wouldn't allow her to disgrace his home and family.

Jason and Paul had both gone out earlier on some undisclosed errand, and Stavros, apparently at a loose end, wandered repeatedly into the kitchen, sampling bits of the food until Voula, scolding gently, shooed him out, telling him to wait on the terrace and she would send Sophie out with coffee for both of them.

Sophie was glad of the opportunity to sit and relax as she joined Stavros with the coffee tray. She sipped with appreciation at the thick, sweet brew, smiling at her father-in-law as he complimented her on the coffee. Then he added, a note of annoyance in his voice, "Why did those boys go off this morning?"

Sophie smiled at the thought of Jason being referred to as a boy. "I suppose they felt they would be in the way." Her face grew serious. "Tell me, *Patera,* what was Jason like as a boy?"

His bright blue eyes regarded her keenly for a long moment, then his thoughts seemed to turn inward, and she waited patiently until at last he spoke.

"We were poor. The whole village was poor. After the Germans left, there was the civil war, an even worse time. The country was already weakened by the world war, then this one dragged on for heartbreaking years, in many cases pitting brother against brother and father against son. We decided it would be best if we left the village and tried to find work in Athens."

He sighed heavily. "There were many times I regretted it. Jobs were hard to find and usually didn't last long. At least in the country we had our garden. Here we had to buy everything. Jason's mother worked scrubbing floors until Paul was born. After that she seemed to lose vitality, probably because of the poor food during her pregnancy. Who knows? She died when Paul was eleven. She never saw our fortunes improve.''

He broke off and was silent for so long that Sophie, seeing the pallor of his skin, began to wish she had not brought up a subject that still had the power to cause him pain. She covered his thin hand with her own. "It's all right, *Patera,*" she said gently. "If it hurts you, let's not talk about it.''

Stavros turned his hand and squeezed her fingers. "Forgive an old man, Sophie. The memories. It was a hard life, but we loved each other." He took a handkerchief from his pocket and blew his nose.

He continued. "Jason started to work when Paul was born. In hotels, restaurants, even in repair garages. He learned his English through contact with the tourists, improving it until he was fluent. He had a flair for machinery and organization, and a likable personality."

This Sophie could believe. When he wanted to, Jason could charm the birds out of the trees, she was willing to concede, even though she had not always been the benefactor of his charm. "Go on," she encouraged Stavros.

"If Jason seems hard now, it's because he never really was a child. The other children were playing with their friends in the street while he was working twelve, sixteen, sometimes eighteen hours a day. Helen was living with us, too, and Jason took care of all of us. His single-minded determination never to be poor and hungry again drove him to make as much money as he could. Anything else took second place. His biggest regret is that the money came too late to save his mother. She needed a serious operation, and our means didn't extend to that. We were only able to move out of our tiny apartment a year after her death. Jason, I think, has never forgiven himself for being too late."

Sophie was silent, wishing she had known all this about her husband earlier—two and a half years earlier. Perhaps she would have been more tolerant when she thought he'd been neglecting her.

Stavros, perhaps divining the direction of her thoughts, patted her knee. "He's a good man, my stubborn Jason. Cherish him, Sophie."

Sophie thought with consternation bordering on panic: *I don't even know if I'll stay with him.* Aloud she merely said, "Yes, *Patera*."

Stavros rose to his feet. "I'll go and see if the mail has come."

Left alone, Sophie studied the sharply defined shadows the overhanging grapevine threw on the white stucco wall. Strange how in Greece the shadows were denser and blacker than any place else in the world. Was the sun brighter, the air clearer? She suddenly knew she would be sorry to leave here. She loved the country and the people, for all their inherent obstinacy and lack of trust in their fellow human beings. If there was any chance that Jason would treat her like a real wife rather than a mere possession, she would stay in a minute. Stavros' words had given her some insight into his complex personality, but where did it leave her? If he could not love her as an equal, she could not bear to live with him.

She rose impatiently—sitting here nursing regrets was getting her nowhere—and began putting the coffee cups on the tray.

Seven

Jason and Sophie stood at the door waiting to greet the first dinner guests, who were due to arrive any moment. Dressed in elegantly cut dinner clothes, Jason looked devastatingly handsome, his face at its most sardonic as he laid his eyes on Sophie for the space of a few seconds. She was beautifully turned out in a gown that he had purchased that morning. Her high color was due to temper, not makeup.

Earlier, in their room, they'd had a flaming row over this very dress, which must have been audible all over the house. Sophie had laid out one of her own dresses, and Jason had sharply vetoed it as too conservative, producing a box from one of the most exclusive dress shops in Kolonaki. She hadn't wanted to accept such an extravagant gift from him under the present circumstances. Until the status of their marriage was clarified, she refused to be dependent upon him in any way.

By sheer strength of will and iron determination, Jason had coerced her into wearing the dress, saying that he would dress her himself if she did not put it on. Not doubting his word, and fearing the touch of his hard hands on her body while she no longer had the will-power to deny that he could arouse her sensual desires, she had given in, but not gracefully.

Jason whispered in her ear at one point in the evening, "You look beautiful, Sophie. I've been complimented several times."

Sophie's teeth set with renewed irritation at the implied reminder that she was a useful and decorative adjunct to his business. She drew her lips back in a brittle smile that anyone watching would have thought entirely genuine. "I hate you," she hissed through angrily clenched teeth.

His smile mocked her. "Keep it up, darling. No one would ever suspect."

"What would you do if I made a scene?" she whispered.

His eyes turned black and dangerous. "Just try it," he grated. Then someone came up and spoke to him, and his party mask fell back into place so quickly it took Sophie's breath away. What an actor the man was. No wonder he had so swiftly risen to the top in the dog-eat-dog world of international commerce.

Sophie was tired by the time the party wound up after midnight, more a weariness of mind than body. It had been a long time since she had entertained on any scale, and she had forgotten the effort it takes to make sure everyone is happy, that no one feels neglected.

Jason helped her carry glasses into the kitchen, emptying ashtrays into a metal bucket with a tight-fitting lid. He did not smoke himself and disliked waking in a smoke-scented house, a principle with which Sophie wholeheartedly agreed.

"The party was perfect, Sophie. I was proud of you." She no longer had the energy to argue with him and took the remark at face value. In any case she could detect neither insincerity nor a patronizing attitude behind his words this time.

"Thank you, Jason. I'm glad everyone had a good time."

"I'm sure they did. Anything else to be done?" Polite, conventional words. Hearing them now, no one would suspect that six hours earlier they had been at each other's throats, saying harsh things that still echoed in Sophie's ears if she allowed herself to dwell on them.

"I can manage. I'll only be a few minutes more. You go up, Jason."

Jason was already in bed when she came up. After a quick shower, she got in beside him. He turned out the lamp, plunging the room into darkness. The shutters were open as Jason liked them, but there was no moon. The heady scent of roses in the garden below the window drifted elusively through the room while crickets shrilled their night music in the cypress tree at the corner of the house.

Sophie had almost drifted into sleep when Jason moved his legs, bringing them closer to her own. Something was different. Sleeping together, some physical contact was unavoidable, but this time instead of the smooth silk of his pajama trousers she encountered the roughness of his hair-sprinkled thigh. She was shocked into full wakefulness. Without conscious volition, desire ran like quicksilver along her veins. She bit her lip until she tasted the salt of her own blood to prevent her traitorous body from turning and burying itself in him.

After an endless moment, pretending sleep, she turned away from him, putting a safe distance between them.

She awoke to find herself clasped against his body, her back to his front, with his arms about her waist. She tried stealthily to move out of his possessive hold, and then she realized he was not sleeping. His breath was warm on her nape as he murmured, "Sophie, don't move."

She struggled against the steel band of his arm. "Jason, let me go," she pleaded desperately, her senses reeling.

"Why?" he whispered provocatively. "You like it."

"I don't!" she exclaimed.

"Yes, you do." His mouth caressed her neck with warm insistence. "When you're sleeping, you come into my arms."

"I don't!" she repeated vehemently, wriggling to free herself but achieving only closer contact with him. She stopped moving as she felt his unmistakable reaction to her movements. At the realization, hot excitement raced through her body even as her conscious mind tried to warn her of danger. She sought refuge in anger.

"Jason, don't you understand that I don't want you anymore, and nothing you do can make me?"

Skillfully he turned her to face him, one hand holding her firmly against his body.

"But I want you," he said against her mouth before kissing her with a fierce, demanding hunger. Sophie, her resolve softened in the aftermath of deep sleep, and seduced by the feel of his hard body and the memory of past love, could not help responding for a wild instant. She was drowning in sweet sensation, but as his hand fell to her thigh and began an unhurried journey upward, an image flashed into her brain, restoring sanity with the force of a dash of cold water.

Jason, thinking she was on the point of capitulation, had relaxed his hold. Evading his grasping hands, Sophie lunged out of the bed, smoothing down her disordered nightdress with shaking hands.

Jason's mocking laughter followed her as she dashed into the bathroom, locking the door. Well might he laugh, she thought as she remembered that the lock did not work. She leaned on the door, half expecting him to force his way in. When she heard nothing from the other room, she ran water into the basin and began to wash her flushed face.

She returned to the bedroom and found Jason out of bed, standing at the open closet door, selecting his clothes for the day. Perhaps as a concession to her modesty, though she doubted it, he was wearing brief undershorts. He said, casually as though nothing had happened—and of course, nothing had, except a further erosion of Sophie's resistance—"I thought we'd go to church, take Father."

"Yes, I'd like that," Sophie said stiffly. At least he wouldn't try to make love to her in church.

The uneasy feeling that Jason was beginning to act on his remark of the night he had torn her clothes remained with Sophie throughout the day like a nagging toothache. He was now trying to reach her through her senses, and this, if he only knew, would reach her far more quickly than any show of force. He abandoned the

sarcasm and cutting remarks with which he had lacer-
ated her emotions in the last weeks, suddenly substitut-
ing a manner that could not have been more solicitous.

Alarm bells were sounding insistently in her mind, but
what could she accuse him of? She could just see the su-
percilious lifting of his brows that would accompany his
comments about her overactive imagination. So she remained silent and watchful.

That evening Sophie was in bed reading when Jason
came up. His eyes flicked over her as he entered the
room, but he said nothing as he went into the bathroom.

Determinedly, Sophie turned back to her book and
shut her ears to the sound of the shower that persisted in
conjuring up a picture of Jason's naked body, the image
imposing itself between her eyes and the printed pages.

She heard the door open and looked up. For a moment he was outlined against the light of the bathroom,
a dark silhouette; then he switched it off. He strode
across the room, magnificent in his unashamed nudity,
a statue of Apollo come to life and endowed with very
human characteristics. Sophie could no longer pretend
to ignore his lack of clothing as she had the previous
night. But before she could speak, Jason, with his almost eerie ability to read her mind, commented as he
pulled the sheet over himself, "I couldn't stand wearing
them any longer. Do you now that I never wore pajamas, even as a kid?" Sophie knew this might have been
because of poverty rather than preference. "I don't even
own any."

Sophie licked her dry lips. "Then whose were those?"

"I borrowed them from Paul." He grinned at her,
correctly interpreting the look on her face. "He doesn't
know I have them. I lifted them from his drawer, and

when the laundry is put back he'll never know they were missing.''

Gently he took the book from her nerveless fingers and laid it on the bedside table. He leaned over her, his hand coming down on the pillow at the opposite side of her head. She gazed up at him, mute, mesmerized by the smoldering passion in his eyes.

"I want you," he whispered, his voice a seduction. "But only when you want me, too."

Sophie swallowed in an effort to moisten her dry mouth. "That day will never come," she said, but her voice lacked the ferocity she had intended.

"We'll see. You wanted me once. You couldn't get enough of me. You'll want me again. You'll be a real wife again." A strange little smile played over his lips, then they were blotted out of her sight as he lowered them to cover hers. He kissed her with exquisite restraint, his mouth soft and warm on hers, tantalizing but never satisfying, until she thought she would go mad.

Just when she was at the breaking point, he raised his head, studying her flushed face as if he wished to memorize every nuance of her features. He pushed the sheet down and ran his hand slowly down her body from breast to thigh and back again. She was unable to prevent a gasp from passing her lips as he lingered fractionally on one breast before reaching out and turning off the lamp.

He lay down, his back to her. "Good night, Sophie." There was an edge of laughter in his voice, and Sophie had an almost uncontrollable urge to pick up the lamp and smash it over his head.

From that night on, the war between them stepped up in intensity, with each side grimly determined to outlast the other. Sophie began sleeping badly, all too aware of Jason's nearness in the bed at night. Dark shadows lay beneath her eyes, which grew as clouded as a stormy sea. Her emotions were feeding on her constantly, and in only one week she was noticeably thinner, weight she could ill afford to lose.

Jason appeared outwardly unchanged, but little things gave him away. He never missed an opportunity to touch her, pushing back a stray lock of hair or adjusting the collar of her dress, and she found herself shrinking away from him whenever he came near her.

Only Stavros seemed to notice nothing amiss; in fact he apparently thought they had made up, especially in view of Jason's solicitous treatment of Sophie in public. She mused at the irony of the situation. If only he knew of the silent battle that went on in their bedroom at night. Jason kissed her and sometimes caressed her until she thought she would scream with frustration. He himself never lost control, although once she had known a grim satisfaction to see sweat standing on his forehead, evidence of what it cost him to arouse her without ever following through to a natural conclusion.

She had given up trying to reason with him, knowing from past experience that once he had determined a course of action, nothing short of an act of God would divert him from it.

Only once did she discover, quite by accident, that the strain was beginning to tell on him. Paul, moving around the dinner table, bumped Jason slightly in passing, and Jason snapped at him irritably, all out of proportion to the minor incident. Paul looked startled, muttering an apology that Jason dismissed with a petulant frown.

Sophie suspected that Jason, having known her so intimately from their first year together, hadn't reckoned with the strength of will she had developed in the last two years. He had expected her to give in before this. The thought made her more determined than ever to hold out until he tired of the game.

By the end of the week, Jason, still polite in public, was snapping at her in private like a dog deprived of a particularly succulent bone. Wisely, Sophie hid her amusement at his behavior. He was used to getting his own way, and when something was denied him, he became childish in a manner she never would have expected from him. Perhaps it was because he had never been a child during childhood—and now had the means to indulge every whim—that it enraged him to be denied something he had set his heart on.

"Congratulate me, Sophie," Paul cried exultantly. He fairly bounded into the living room, brandishing a green bottle with bright foil at the neck. He crossed the room to the china cabinet and extracted two stemmed glasses. "The very best champagne." He yanked out the cork with a carelessness that would have horrified the vintner and barely caught the foaming liquid in the glass.

Sophie, laughing in a rather bewildered fashion, took a glass from him. "What are we celebrating?"

He blew on his fingernails and pretended to dust them on his shirtfront. "I've been made the regional manager of Stephanou Industries for all of Greece."

For a moment Sophie was speechless with surprise. Was Jason at last delegating some of his formidable workload? "So Jason finally recognized your worth."

For a moment Paul looked faintly worried, as though the enormity of his new responsibilities had just struck him. Then with typical exuberance, his face cleared. "Not only that," he said. "Jason appointed managers for all the areas of the company he formerly looked after on his own: shipping, electronics, manufacturing. Of course we're all accountable to him, but it seems he's planning to slow down." He looked speculatively at Sophie. "You wouldn't have had something to do with that, would you?"

"Me? Hardly." But Jason's sudden departure from his single-minded attendance to business disturbed her more than she let on. What did it mean? She shrugged off the feeling, raising her glass and touching it to the rim of Paul's. "Much luck in your new job, Paul."

"Thanks. I'm afraid I'll need it." He swallowed the contents of his glass, then refilled it. "Come on, Sophie, drink up."

By the time Jason came home an hour later, both of them were pleasantly tipsy, laughing together like a couple of kids. Storm clouds gathered in Jason's eyes as he saw them sprawled in two chairs with Sophie's dress riding up above her knees. But Paul averted the threatened thunder and lightning by grabbing Jason's hand and shaking it vigorously.

"Thanks, big brother," he said as seriously as he could after half a bottle of champagne in the middle of the afternoon. "I won't let you down."

"You'd better believe I won't let you," Jason said, but he smiled with unusual warmth as he took a glass and drank a toast to Paul.

"I've decided to take a holiday of a week or so," Jason announced that night. He pulled a familiar dark blue object out of the drawer beside him. "By the way, here's your passport. Since you find it difficult to take things from me, use it to cash some travelers' checks if you need clothes or anything."

Sophie, seated at her dressing table, paused in the act of drawing the brush through her hair. He met her eyes in the mirror as he lay on the bed watching her. "Does this mean you're going to let me go back to Vancouver?" she asked, carefully keeping her voice neutral.

His mouth curved in a smile that was meant to disarm her, but his eyes remained hard and cold. "No, you're going with me on my holiday."

Sophie swung around on the stool. "Jason, isn't it enough? You've been keeping me here against my will, forcing me to be close to you, taking away all my privacy. Can't you stop tormenting me? There's nothing left."

"Isn't there?" he drawled, a savage glitter coming into his eyes. He swung his legs off the bed and stood up.

Sophie caught her breath at the sight of his bare body, then resolutely damped down the fire that rose in her, turning back to the mirror. He came toward her, his bare feet silent, almost stealthy on the thick carpet. He grasped her shoulders, the pressure of his hands firm but not hard enough to hurt her. She regarded him fearfully in the glass. The smooth skin of his shoulders gleamed like old gold in the lamplight, his face in shadow wearing a hard look. Her heart was thundering in her ears so loudly she wondered if he could hear it.

He lowered his head and put his mouth to the smooth skin at the side of her neck, brushing her hair to one side with gentle fingers. The tip of his tongue trailed liquid fire in its wake, causing an involuntary shudder to shake her whole body.

"Give in, Sophie. Wouldn't it be easier to give in and relieve the ache?" His voice was husky, barely audible even this close.

"No," she blurted. "Never!" She wrenched herself free of his hands and resumed brushing her hair. Jason took the brush from her shaking hand and ran it through the long, lustrous mane.

"Such lovely hair," he murmured. "Like captured moonlight. When you were away I used to dream about your hair spread out on the pillow, and about how soft your skin was, and how I wanted to touch you, in all your secret places. When will you let me again, Sophie?" His voice was soft and hypnotic, and Sophie's bones turned into hot liquid. For a moment she was afraid she would faint, as all the blood seemed to rush from her brain to gather in a molten pool in the center of her. She shut her eyes so tightly it hurt, as if she could shut out his words as well as the sight of him.

If he only knew how she longed to give herself totally to him. Day by day it was becoming increasingly difficult for her to hold on to her principles, for her not to give in to the gnawing ache inside her that only his complete possession could assuage.

She was so tired, and leaned against him for a moment, opening her eyes and seeing the silvery strands of her hair mingling with the mat of black hair on his chest. The heavy beat of his heart seeped into her until it synchronized with hers. Her eyelids dropped over her eyes, hiding her languorous expression from his all-seeing gaze.

"Sophie?" Jason murmured questioningly.

She came out of the trance, rising swiftly and getting into bed. "Good night, Jason." Two could play that game too. Then why did she feel so flat, with no satisfaction at paying him back in his own coin?

Jason was already dressed when she awoke in the morning. He was pushing up the knot of his tie in front of the mirror. Seeing her reflection, her eyes open and warily fixed on him, his mobile mouth quirked slightly, but he said nothing. He shrugged into his jacket, checking the pockets for keys.

He sat down on the edge of the bed, his two hands coming around her head. He threaded his fingers through her hair, molding the delicate shape of her skull. His thumbs moved back and forth on her pink-flushed cheeks.

"So beautiful in the morning, Sophie," he whispered, and there was no mockery in his voice. The tenderly passionate look in his dark eyes sent a lightning flash of desire through her, and it was all she could do not to cry out: *Take me, Jason. Love me.*

Only the memory of his implacable possessiveness saved her. This was the look she had always found impossible to resist. It had always worked for him, but now she couldn't let it.

Yet when his mouth came down in a kiss of scalding hunger, she opened her mouth to receive it, knowing his office at this time of day pulled him more strongly than she was ever likely to.

Lifting his head, he muttered thickly, "You almost tempt me to stay." Sophie could feel his fingers trembling until he tightened them in her hair. She could not stop herself from bending her head for greater contact with his hand, but perhaps he didn't notice, as he added, "But not yet, my lovely witch. Not yet." Slowly, reluctantly, he released her.

As soon as he was out of the room, Sophie let out a long, ragged breath. Tears that seemed so near the surface these days filled her eyes. She turned over, burying her face in the pillow—the same pillow where Jason had slept, still fragrant with his clean body scent.

If only he loved her as well as desired her. If only she could trust him to allow her to keep her self.

Two days later they were in the Jaguar speeding along the straight road that ran from Athens to the Corinth Canal. The miles passed swiftly, in virtual silence except for the hum of the engine.

Laura had phoned that morning to tell Sophie the clothes had arrived. "They're wonderful," she said, bubbling with enthusiasm. "Can you get more?"

"I've got more on order," Sophie told her.

Which meant that her business would prosper. But what about her marriage?

Sophie had been entertaining the thought that on this break from business pressures Jason would let down his barriers and reveal his real feelings about her and their marriage instead of skating around the edges of the issue as he had done for days. She could not shake off an impression, more of an intuition really, that Jason was fighting some inner battle. His fluctuating moods, one moment threatening, the next making heartbreakingly tender love to her, all pointed to a man torn within himself.

At the moment, she could discern nothing from his expression. He propelled the powerful car along the road with awesome confidence, but driving could have been the only thing on his mind for all the information his face gave away. He glanced over at her, his eyes dark and brooding, lightening only as a faint smile touched his lips.

"Are you all right, Sophie?"

She sighed. "I'm okay." Then to fill the silence she said, "It was nice of you to give Paul a promotion."

Jason shrugged. "He's intelligent enough if he applies himself. I expect him to do well. At least it'll keep him too busy to fool around."

"And you'll have more leisure time."

His eyes remained fixed on the road. "Yes. About time, don't you think? I won't be the neglectful husband who is always away, as I was before." His tone was very faintly sarcastic.

Sophie had no reply to this, although her mind started busily worrying this over. Had he done it for her? She didn't dare to believe it. There had to be a catch.

Unknowingly giving a heavy sigh, she turned her head to stare out the window at the scenery flying by.

They passed through the outer edges of Corinth, taking the narrow and winding road toward Mycenae, crossing and recrossing the railroad that served the Peloponnese. It was a golden September morning, and the landscape around them was beautiful, appealing to all the senses. Citrus groves stretched on either side of the road, the trees showing green fruit between the abundant glossy foliage. Interspersed with them were other fruit trees and the inevitable vineyards, the small grapevines heavy with ripe fruit.

They spent an hour or two at Mycenae, admiring the symmetrical circle graves where archaeologists had unearthed fabulous treasure, surely beyond even their wildest dreams. Sophie had visited the site before, but she was astonished anew at the massive stone walls and gates surmounted by solid stones weighing over a hundred tons each, all erected without the aid of modern machinery.

Jason was surprisingly knowledgeable about ancient history, considering that he had spent the greater part of his childhood working. He must have studied later to make up for his lack of formal education. How little she really knew about him. Had she been so young when they married that it hadn't mattered? Perhaps that was why he had never shared his past or discussed his future dreams and aspirations with her. She had probably given him the impression she didn't care. But was it too late now to make amends?

Leaving the car in the central parking lot, they walked to the beehive tomb outside the main citadel. There were few other sightseers there. Voices bounced from the smooth masonry walls inside the cone-shaped structure, echoing and re-echoing eerily.

One man who had a lighter led the way into the second room, which was smaller and completely dark. Suddenly the light went out, plunging the chamber into a blackness that could almost be felt. The small group stood, scarcely breathing. No one spoke and the only light came from a couple of sparks as the man attempted to relight the lighter.

Sophie suddenly realized that Jason was not beside her. Already nervy from tension and lack of sleep, she was gripped by panic that caught her throat in a vise. She couldn't breathe. She couldn't see. This must be what it was like to be blind. Maybe she was. No place on earth could be this dark.

She opened her mouth to scream, but no sound came out. Turning, she looked frantically for the opening to the other room. She came in contact with a solid wall, and another scream arose in her throat. The wall was warm, moving toward her, and with overwhelming relief she recognized the scent of Jason's aftershave. He put his arms around her, and without thought of possible consequences she buried her face against his hard chest, gulping air into her lungs.

He lifted her chin with warm fingers and kissed her mouth. Sophie, in her distressed state, had no resistance to the seductive pressure of his lips and hard body. She responded as she had been longing to do, and a sweetness shafted through her with an intensity that was almost pain.

The moment shattered when someone came in with a lighted candle. Everyone filed out into the main chamber, chattering over-loudly in their relief. The entire incident had lasted only two minutes, yet it seemed an age had passed.

Outside in the hot sunlight, Sophie cast Jason a sidelong glance as they threaded their way through a group of noisy tourists coming off a tour bus. His face was wearing its inscrutable mask, giving no sign that he had been moved. Yet she could not restrain a quiver of excitement. In a few hours it would be night, they would be alone together in the hotel room, and anything might happen. Could she lower her pride and meet him halfway? Could she settle for a lifetime with this man, knowing he did not love her? Would her love be enough for both of them? She dared not think that far ahead.

Overnight they stayed in Sparta at a hotel in the modern town center. The beds were twins, to Sophie's mixed relief and disappointment. Jason seemed to have forgotten the kiss in the tomb, or perhaps he regretted his lapse from formality. At any rate, he made no move to take up from where they had left off.

It took Sophie a very long time to fall asleep.

The greater part of the following day was spent exploring the Byzantine ruins at Mystra. Jason again treated Sophie more like a sister than a wife, and Sophie was obscurely disappointed, though she was careful to hide it from him. The barrier remained between them, as impenetrable as ever.

From Sparta to Kalamata the road ran through some of the most spectacular scenery in Greece—heavily forested mountains and awesome gorges, some with threadlike rivers barely visible in their depths and an occasional tiny arched stone mule bridge crossing the torrent of water, far below the modern highway bridge. Mount Taygetos reared up in the near distance, its summit crowned by swirling black clouds that descended at intervals to release some of their moisture, conveying a welcome coolness to the hot afternoon.

The hotel in Kalamata was situated on the sea front. One had only to cross the road and descend a short flight of steps to be on the shingle beach where an incredibly blue ocean washed its lacy edges, its color pale at the shore and deepening to a dense purple in the distance—Homer's wine-dark sea.

While Jason was showering in the bathroom that adjoined their room, Sophie changed into a long white dress of filmy cotton gauze that was loose and cool yet revealed more of her slender figure than was apparent

at first glance. Her feelings of excitement and anticipation were stronger than ever.

In the bathroom, when Jason was through, she applied makeup lightly, although she needed little artifi-
cial enhancement. Her eyes sparkled, and her cheeks
were already flushed with becoming color.

She came out of the bathroom to find Jason fully
dressed, in black trousers that fit snugly to his lean hips
and muscular thighs and a black silk shirt unbuttoned
nearly to the waist. The darkness of the clothes gave him
the appearance of a pirate. His dark blue eyes moved
slowly over her, but his expression did not alter.

''Ready?'' he asked.

At her nod he took her arm, and they went downstairs and out in the warm, fragrant evening.

The town with its citrus trees and palm-lined streets
had an almost tropical air, while retaining the vitality
that is peculiarly Greek. After walking for a time they sat
down at a seaside *taverna*. Jason ordered food and a delicious white wine that still held the heady fragrance of
sun-warmed grapes. They ate delectable deep-fried baby
squids and lamb chops flavored with garlic and lemon.
The wine seemed to go to Sophie's head even though she
drank only sparingly of it. Or perhaps it was the surroundings, the sense of freedom and expectancy that
pervaded her being, enhancing the flavor of the food and
drink.

Jason maintained his aloof air; yet when she looked
at him unexpectedly his eyes were on her, their blue filled
with mysterious shadows, dark and unfathomable as
night skies.

Something had changed between them. It wasn't just
the fact that they were on their own, away from work and

family. It had started in Athens, perhaps on the night he had announced the forthcoming holiday, and Mycenae had intensified the strange feeling of anticipation, of some momentous event waiting to happen. An almost breathless excitement lay between them. She wondered if Jason were as aware of it as she was. One could never figure out what he was thinking behind those dark eyes of his. She only knew that her resistance was at its lower ebb, the kiss in Mycenae having burned away the final vestiges of her opposition.

She was ready to surrender. The only question was when. Jason had to make the first move, and when he did, she would not refuse.

Perhaps tonight.

Eight

The fine, smooth pebbles of the beach still retained the heat of the sunny afternoon, and Sophie gloried in the warm feel of them against her bare feet. She carried her sandals in one hand and Jason held the other, his long fingers twined lightly between hers. Overhead the moon sailed high, transformed from the orange globe that had risen as they ate their meal into a white lantern, shedding its cool light on the beach, illuminating each separate stone so that it glittered like a precious jewel.

Jason's hand was warm, sending a tingle up her arm. Her head felt light, as if she had consumed too much wine. She knew she hadn't—it was something in the very air, an anticipation of she knew not what. The hour was late and they were alone on the beach, the moon trailing her luminous skirts in the calm water that whispered mysteriously, kissing the sand at its border.

Sophie glanced back toward the town. Thick shadows lay between the buildings, the moonlight brighter than the street lamps. The houses were dark and shuttered. Even in the hotels few lights glowed, the occupants of the rooms having long since succumbed to sleep.

Their steps became slower and slower. Sophie felt as though she were walking in a dream, divorced from reality. The scent of citrus leaves and eucalyptus mixed with the heavy perfume of gardenias drifted down from the upper slopes of the town, an intoxicating, potent aphrodisiac.

As they reached the shadow of a great plane tree that overhung the beach, Jason without a word took her in his arms and covered her mouth in a kiss that started out to be tender but quickly deepened into a burning, hungering passion. Sophie responded with all the fervor of long pent-up emotion. Her sandals fell unnoticed to the ground as she put her arms about his neck, holding him close, her fingers tangled in the sensuously silky hair at the back of his head. He pulled her against his hard body, and she bonelessly molded herself to him. She felt faint, trembling on the edge of a vortex that threatened to pull her under, her mind whirling with sensations too long denied.

Jason raised his head and she could see the hard planes of his face taut with emotion, the blue eyes black in the moonlight. "Sophie," he murmured, "tell me what you want."

Sophie had only to say the words to project them beyond the point of no return, yet for an instant habit revived, allowing a last pocket of resistance to manifest itself. A tight muscle at at the corner of Jason's mouth showed her that the struggle must be evident in the look in her eyes. She lowered her lashes, concealing them from his unblinking scrutiny. "I want you," she whispered, her voice so thick she could hardly speak.

He became so still that at last she was forced to look up. The moonlight had altered subtly, leaching the colors out of all objects it touched. Jason's face was white, the skin stretched tight over the bones, the eyes black holes. This was what he would look like if he were dead. She shuddered convulsively, unable to bear the thought of being in a world in which he did not exist. Even if happiness for her lasted only this one night, she had to have that night.

"Jason, take me," she cried softly. "I want you now." Her voice was stronger and he accepted her surrender, the coiled tension leaving his body.

There were no words of love, but the stark need she saw in his eyes and knew within herself had to be satisfied. Perhaps there would never be love—unless she could convey her own love to him in the joining of their bodies.

Jason stooped to pick up her sandals and she walked quietly beside him to the hotel, refusing to dwell on the future beyond this magic night. If it was only moon madness, she would at least have this to remember through the lonely years to come.

She never remembered afterward how they reached the hotel room, only that they didn't meet a soul. If they had, she probably wouldn't have noticed.

Jason closed and locked the door, then came slowly across the floor to her, treading lightly as though he feared a sudden move would startle her into flight. He did not kiss her, but she could hear the loud thudding of his heart—or was it her own?—as he slid the straps of her dress down over her arms, and let the garment fall in a pool around her feet. She stood shivering in the heat of the room, clad only in her white lace bikini pants. His eyes held hers, seeming to delve into her very soul as he stripped them off and gently laid her on the bed.

He began to undress—first his shirt and trousers, hanging them with elaborate care over a chair, then his shoes and socks, and finally his shorts. She had seen him naked many times in the last week, yet there was something so incredibly erotic in actually watching him undress that her mouth was desert-dry, her heart pounding with intolerable excitement, sending the blood flowing like molten lava through her veins.

He came toward the bed, and she was suddenly more nervous than on her wedding night. "Turn out the light," she begged as his eyes devoured her.

But Jason could not forgive so easily. "No, I want to see you." His voice was thick and harsh, as if he had an obstruction in his throat.

He lay down beside her, gathering her close to him. He still did not kiss her or even caress her. Now that she had given in, it seemed enough to lie pressed together, absorbing the essence of each other through only the touch of their skin.

At last he moved, when her senses were pitched so high that she wondered how she could stand it another second. He began to stroke his hands down her body, caressing her until all her skin was glowing with an unquenchable fire. Then he kissed her, exploring her mouth as though it were a land of indescribable beauty that he had to savor to the full. She tasted the sweetness of his mouth, thinking she would never have enough of it. His tongue trailed hotly over her flushed cheeks to the hollow of her throat, lingering there, then moving back up to the sensitive lobe of her ear. He whispered, his warm breath feathering her skin, "Tell me what you want me to do."

She surfaced slightly, confused, her surrender too recent to have brought back ease of communication. "No," she said in a small shaken voice, "I can't."

"Yes, you can," he said implacably. "I want you to tell me what you like, or we'll stop this now." He shifted so that no part of him touched her. "I want you to beg." Then, suddenly, he groaned, "No, I need you too much."

As if driven by demons he reached for her and at the same time she flung herself against him in reckless abandon. "Jason," she cried frantically. "Touch me, make love to me."

A peculiar groan of triumph passed his lips before they took hers in a searing kiss that held passion, longing and not a little anger as though he felt compelled to punish her for making him wait so long. He was hurting her, but strangely she welcomed the rough strength of him, and her remaining inhibitions fled.

He held her head between his two hands, gently now, as he kissed her yet again, his mouth scalding on her face, his tongue tasting her, drinking her, mating with her tongue. "Sophie, my Sophie," he cried softly. "How could I have been so long without you?"

Sophie, almost out of her mind with the pleasure his hands and his mouth were giving her, barely heard the words. She was long past coherent thought. It didn't matter if he loved her or hated her or if he hated himself for wanting her. She wanted him desperately, his anguished cries and the silken feel of him against her, arousing her to a fever pitch she knew had to end soon.

The room was silent except for their rapid hoarse breathing, words fading to incoherent murmurs. Sophie felt an agonizing pressure building in her as those hard, warm hands—strange yet so familiar, as though her skin had never forgotten their intoxicating touch—continued to caress her with long, silken movements. In a frenzy she writhed against him. "Jason, Jason, please!"

His touch became lighter, a butterfly's breath, soft as rose petals falling to the ground. "Softly, softly, my darling," he breathed, but she was beyond hearing.

"I—can't—wait," she gasped, her hands clawing frantically at his shoulders, her body arching against the hard muscled length of his. He fell over the edge of control and could not withhold himself from her any longer. She saw his face urgent with desire, the blue eyes glazed, his mind centered on one object—their mutual fulfillment. He possessed her at last with a deep, piercing pleasure that sent waves of sensation rolling over her entire body.

He groaned against her throat as he paused for an instant. "It's been so long, so very long—" He cried out her name as he wrung from her an anguished response that had her gasping for breath, her throat burning with unshed tears.

They lay tangled together like survivors of a shipwreck washed up on a beach. Gradually their breathing quieted, but Jason remained lying with his dark head a sweet, heavy weight on her breast. They slept closely entwined until the sun slanted through the open window.

The lamp, forgotten, glowed a sickly yellow, its feeble light eclipsed by the power of the sun.

Sophie came half awake, snuggling closer to the solid warmth beside her, then suddenly coming to full consciousness. She turned her head and looked at Jason, his tousled hair dark against the white pillow. His face was relaxed in sleep, the dark lashes lying on his cheeks—so long and curling they would have been the envy of any woman, faintly incongruous with his tough features. A tender smile curved her mouth. She wanted to wake him, and yet she didn't. It was a pleasure for her to feast her eyes on him while he slept, his guard down, unconscious of her scrutiny. For a few heady moments, he belonged entirely to her.

Was he really as tough as he looked? How she wished there were better communication between them, that he would talk to her. She sighed heavily, the smile gone. He had been self-reliant and independent almost from infancy. How could he change now?

Yet her soul ached to be one with him, going beyond a oneness of the body.

His eyes opened and she flushed, embarrassed that she had been caught staring at him. She turned, reaching for her light dressing gown. Jason snaked out one long arm and pulled her against him before she could succeed in the maneuver.

"Sophie," he murmured seductively, his strong white teeth nibbling at her ear. "Once wasn't enough for me, and I'm sure it wasn't enough for you after all this time."

She made no reply, merely burying her face in the hollow of his shoulder. He laughed shortly and triumphantly as his hands began to caress her, slowly and languidly until she was half delirious with the sensual pleasure he was arousing in her. She opened her eyes once and saw his face, absorbed but without the hunger it had evidenced last night, curiously detached as though he knew the pleasure he was giving her but was receiving none himself.

She shut her eyes, erasing the image, her heart contracting with pain, though it was not enough to bring her to cold sanity. He was still punishing her, but the thought did not take firm hold until later when she lay sated in his arms.

Only the knowledge that at the last minute he had thrown off his detachment and had attained the heights of rapture with her relieved the ache in her soul.

Jason, seemingly unaware of the conflicting emotions within her, smiled lazily. "We used to spend all our time making love, didn't we?"

Sophie pulled herself out of his arms and succeeded in putting on her robe. Her face averted, she replied, "Maybe that was the trouble. We never took the time to talk."

She arose swiftly to her feet, moving toward the bathroom, but not before she sensed that he stiffened. She did not turn to look whether her shaft had driven home.

"Are you ready?" Jason asked later as he came out of the bathroom after his shower. He took in her sundress of brightly printed cotton with saucy bows at the shoulders. "Are you going like that? We're only going on a picnic. Why don't you wear shorts?"

"Okay," Sophie said with determined cheer. "Go on and load the car. I'll be right down."

When she went out ten minutes later, the picnic basket packed by the hotel kitchen rested on the rear seat of the Jaguar, and Jason stood beside the car talking with some people who were waiting for a tour bus. He detached himself from the group as soon as he saw her, grinning with approval at her white shorts and blue camisole T-shirt. She blushed slightly, wondering if he noticed that on a last-minute impulse she had left off her bra. He must have, for under his interested gaze her nipples tingled and stood erect, plainly visible through the fine cotton knit.

He laughed as he helped her into the low car, whispering in her ear as he closed the door, "Let's go before I change my mind and take you back to bed."

They drove into the hills, taking a rough road that led to a high plateau. In the distance far below, the sea shimmered in the sun, alive with light and color, the nourishing lifeblood of the country for centuries.

"I was stationed here for a time during my military service," Jason told her. "We marched in these hills all one summer. Talk about heat! We'd sweat so much we could pour the water out of our boots at the end of the day."

They left the car and walked to a sheltered cup in a grassy meadow. Far away on the shrubby mountainside, sheep bells tinkled, faint music that hadn't changed since the time of Pericles.

As they ate their lunch, they talked lightly of inconsequential matters, but Sophie felt ill at ease under her bright smile. She could not rid herself of the image of his face that morning, cold and hard while his hands caressed her. It seemed indelibly printed on her mind, like an icy specter taking the heat and the enjoyment from the day.

After they had cleared away the leftover food and packed the dishes back into the basket, they lay back on the blanket, drowsily content. The sun was hot and enervating, and Sophie closed her eyes, turning her face up to the cobalt sky, reveling in the warmth. She was a true sun-worshiper without carrying it to the extreme of damaging her skin. Jason had removed his shirt and jeans and wore only the swimming trunks he had had on underneath. He lay on his side, elbow on the ground, his head propped up on his hand.

Reaching over with the other hand, he traced his forefinger down Sophie's nose. "Why so pensive, Sophie? What are you thinking?"

She was reluctant to tell him, then decided it might open up an avenue of communication. "How it was in the beginning. The island. Our honeymoon." She suddenly smiled. "Remember how I slipped on the rocks and got all covered with seaweed?"

Jason laughed, carefree for once without any tension. "Yes, like an extremely untidy mermaid. And when I laughed you pulled me in, clothes and all." He sobered, cupping his hand around her cheek. "Sophie, it could be like that again."

"No, it couldn't," Sophie said sadly. "I'm not the same person."

"Are any of us? We all change, but that doesn't mean we can't have good times again."

Sophie had no reply to this. Then, after a slight pause, she asked, "Why now, Jason? Why did you send for me now? It's been two years. Why not six months ago, or when my father died, or any other time? And don't say because of Stavros. I know that was only an excuse. You knew I would come for him."

Jason sat up, clasping his hands around his bent knees and staring out over the little meadow. "I was in Vancouver on business. I saw you, quite by coincidence, about a week before I sent for you. In a Greek restaurant with some fellow with glasses."

Robert, Sophie thought. It had to have been Robert, a young English professor at the university whom she had been seeing on a fairly regular basis for the past six months.

"Who was he, Sophie?" Jason asked, turning his head to look at her.

"Just a friend," she said, sounding unintentionally defensive.

"Does he know you're married?"

"Of course he does. We're friends. Friends talk to each other."

" 'Friends' covers a lot of territory these days," Jason said sardonically. "Is he your lover?"

"Of course not," Sophie retorted. "I told you I had no lovers."

"You could have lied."

"Well, I didn't."

Jason lay down again, turning over on his stomach and picking up a twig that he idly flicked at a clump of grass. "No, you didn't," he said after a moment. "Last night you felt like a woman who hadn't been with a man for a good long time—like two years."

A curl of warmth awakened in her loins at his words. He had truly aroused the long-suppressed hunger in her, and she knew why she had been able to suppress it. The hunger was only for Jason.

"I saw you in the restaurant, and I made sure you didn't see me," Jason went on in a low voice. "I watched you, and you didn't seem very loverlike toward this man, although I could see he would have liked to be toward you. I figured I'd gotten over you, but that night I couldn't get your face out of my mind. I went home to Athens, but it nagged me until I could hardly sleep. So I sent the telegram."

Sophie had nothing to say. It didn't mean he loved her. Desire was often as strong as love, and could be a more powerful obsession. Also, knowing Jason's past behavior, she suspected jealousy of Robert probably had also motivated his action.

"You must have suspected I might have been behind the telegram," Jason added. "So why did you come?"

"As you figured, Jason." She gave a heavy sigh. "For Stavros. My father was gone. I couldn't just sit by and not go see Stavros if there was a possibility he might die."

"Pray God he'll have many years yet," Jason said seriously. He rolled over until he was right next to her. "But admit it, Sophie," he said with a beguiling smile, "you must have been curious to see me again, too."

The sweetness of the smile took away all her misgivings for the moment. "You have an inflated opinion of your attraction, Jason," she said lightly.

"No, you're the attractive one, Sophie." He squirmed forward until he was leaning over her, his face close to hers. "You're beautiful lying here in the sun," he whispered huskily, his eyes on her soft, pink mouth. "You should always be in the sun. Or in the moonlight in that filmy white dress you wore last night."

He was weaving the sensuous spell again. Sophie caught her breath, waiting, anticipating, yearning for his kiss, but instead of covering her mouth he put his lips against the hollow of her throat where a pulse beat wildly under the pale gold skin.

She clasped her hands together in his crisp black hair, holding him close to her. His hair was warm from the sun, incredibly sensuous against her palms. He moved lower, his mouth nuzzling at her breast, tugging at the nipple through the thin cotton of her camisole. With nimble fingers he unfastened the tiny buttons that closed the front of it, then pushed the edges to the side, baring her small, pointed breasts that strained toward him.

"Beautiful," he murmured, cupping one in his hand, a perfect fit to his palm. "Beautiful and delicious." He tasted them, running his tongue first around one pink nipple, then the other until Sophie felt she would go crazy. She tried to still the little whimpers coming from her throat, but failed completely. Her hands clenched in his hair, then on his shoulders.

Jason, lifting his head and seeing the desperate hunger in her face, the flush on her cheeks, laughed softly. "Don't worry, Sophie. No one can hear you." He chuckled again. "Except me. And I don't mind a bit. Scream if you want. All those little sounds you make just drive me crazy."

While he was talking he was busily unzipping her shorts and sliding them and her underwear off. The hot sun on her bare skin was so exquisitely erotic that she could not help stretching and then relaxing with the fluid grace of a young cat.

Jason kissed her mouth, hungrily, with a passion she responded to with all the recently awakened needs in her. His hands were stroking over her skin, gently, then firmly, then gently again, arousing but never satisfying, until she was writhing under them, twisting herself closer to him.

Abruptly he rolled onto his back, grinning mischievously at her, looking younger than she had ever seen him.

"Jason," she cried in outrage, "you can't stop now."

"Only for a moment." He laughed at her expression, but gently, without any mockery. "It's your turn now."

She managed to arrange her liquid bones and muscles back into a semblance of solidity and sat up. Gazing intently at his reclining body, her eyes lingering on the swim trunks that appeared to have shrunk alarmingly, she murmured impishly, "You don't need any help."

"But it's such fun, Sophie. Take them off."

She did, but not immediately. First she caressed him ever so lightly with only the tips of her fingers, slowly increasing the pressure until she was using her whole hands. She kissed him lightly on the mouth, progressing with maddening stealth down his body, pausing at his nipples half hidden in thick black fur, then trailing moistly down his flat, hard stomach, kissing his navel.

Jason convulsively arched his back toward her. "Sophie," he groaned, almost beside himself. "Do you know what you're doing?"

Sophie laughed, reveling in the power she had over him, for once having the upper hand. "Driving you crazy, Jason, that's what I'm doing."

He gave an indistinct moan as she hooked her fingers in the elastic of his swimsuit and slowly peeled it off. A long ragged gasp shivered in her throat at the sight of him, the awesome masculinity of him. She was half frightened at the extent of his response to her, at the primitive force she had unleashed in him.

When she touched him, a long shudder ran through his body and he clutched her shoulders, gasping, "Sophie, oh Sophie.'' One hand tangled in her hair as he pulled her down to him, their open mouths mating in a heated fusion that sent Sophie spinning into a whirl-pool of drowning pleasure.

Now Jason took over, rolling her onto her back. His hands were trembling as they moved over her in long, sensuous caresses. Then his mouth followed the paths they had blazed, licking, nuzzling, nibbling, at her breasts, her belly, even her hipbones, an astonishingly erotic area she had never before discovered. He slid far-ther down, kissing her knees and working his way slowly back up her legs. Gently his warm hands coaxed her legs apart, the tip of his tongue delicately exploring the vel-vet insides of her thighs, moving slowly higher.

Sophie, almost lost in a haze of sweet sensation, gasped, ''Jason, you can't—ahhh—''

''Can't I?'' he muttered hoarsely, his breath warm against the most sensitive part of her.

She gave a long keening cry and exploded into a mil-lion fragments of ecstasy. Sobbing for breath, half fainting, she lay in Jason's arms as he held her against him, stroking her hair and her face until she sighed, ''So delicious. But what about you?''

''Don't worry,'' he said with that sweet, quirking smile. ''We're not done yet.''

He kissed her deeply, awakening new fires in her. Again he caressed her until a new pressure began build-ing inside her, begging release.

''Now, Jason, now,'' she groaned urgently against his mouth.

''Yes, now,'' he gasped. And he was inside her with all his strength, his powerful movements lifting her once more until together they soared free through layers of ravishing enchantment to burst at last into the sunshine at the peak of the highest ecstasy two people could attain.

"Ah, Sophie," Jason said a long time later when their blood had cooled, their heartbeats slowed, and they could talk once more. "How could you throw this away? This marvelous, wondrous thing between us?"

But she had no answer, her mind confused as it had never been. Sensuality. A profound pleasure almost beyond bearing that touched not only her body but invaded her mind, her heart, her soul. Love.

But was it love on his part? And could she settle for less?

"Jason," she said later as they were driving back toward the hotel. "I have to go back to my shop. I can't let Laura run it alone for much longer."

Jason's face as he glanced at her was expressionless.

"So nothing's changed." He sounded flat and discouraged—or was that a product of the barely fledged hope in her?

Sophie smiled and laid her hand on his thigh, where he covered it with his.

"I could go next week. And I could come back for Christmas, if you want me to, Jason. I need to go," she added, an unconscious plea in her voice. "I have to think about this, about us. I can't make any promises."

He squeezed her hand tightly, bringing it up to his mouth and kissing the palm with the same thoroughness with which he would have kissed her mouth.

"Just as long as you make the right decision, Sophie."

But what was the right decision for her, she wondered as she lay awake late that night listening to Jason's quiet

breathing beside her. She yearned for him with every fi-
ber of her woman's soul, and yet she was still afraid to
trust a future with him.

Nine

The village, many of its houses without glass in the windows, like vacant eyes, staggered up a precipitous cliffside. A square tower dominated the scene, its bulk dwarfing even the simple bell tower of the tiny church. A row of slender cypresses marked the cemetery, their sharp tops thrusting into the cloudless azure sky, uncaring of the bodies buried with profound mourning at their feet.

Sophie shivered despite the heat as the Jaguar passed under the shadow of the fighting tower. Even at noon the densely black area of shade seemed to overpower the houses, giving the scene a sinister, brooding air that was not dispelled by the dilapidated condition of the building's crumbling walls.

Jason stopped the car in the square where the church presided over one end. Old men drinking coffee and thimbles of *ouzo* gazed curiously at the luxurious vehicle that intruded incongruously into this scene of poverty. The proprietor of the *kafenion* came out the door, standing with his hands folded under the incredibly dirty apron that covered his ample waist. He stared at Jason without recognition.

"He recently took over the shop when the previous owner died," Jason murmured to Sophie.

One of the old men waved and Jason walked to the table to have a word with him. Sophie, standing beside the car, glanced about the square. It was depressingly bare, with a few shops around its perimeter, half of them apparently closed.

How did people survive in this desolate place?

A movement between two derelict buildings caught her eye. An old woman, her head enveloped in a black scarf that covered the lower half of her face, leaving only the glittering eyes visible, peeped furtively around the corner of one building. As Sophie's gaze swiveled to her, she took fright, scuttling out of sight up the narrow lane.

Jason came back, and they began to walk up a rough track composed of broken stones, winding between walls of low whitewashed cottages, many of which no longer had the pristine appearance that was usual in Greece. The street was hot and airless, and Sophie had the eerie feeling that unseen eyes were watching them from behind the partially shuttered windows.

"Is your aunt expecting us?" she asked in an attempt to shake off her uneasiness. She chided herself for being fanciful, yet it seemed that invisible ghosts walked here even in the noonday sun.

"No," Jason replied, apparently oblivious to the atmosphere. Why shouldn't he be? He had been born here, played in these streets when he was a tousle-haired little boy in ragged shorts. "She doesn't have a telephone."

"Where is everybody?"

Jason shrugged. "Probably eating their lunch or sleeping. There are few people here now, and most of them are old."

"Where have they gone?" asked Sophie. She stumbled on the sharp edge of a stone in the path, and Jason tucked her arm under his, holding her hand.

"Careful, Sophie." He smiled, glancing down at her flimsy sandals. "Those shoes weren't made for mountain climbing. The people? Many have emigrated, to Canada or to Australia. Some live in that last village we passed through. It's larger, with more amenities."

They had almost reached the top of the town. Above them hundreds of thick, gnarled olive trees, their leaves silvery green against the molten blue of the sky, eked out their existence in the inhospitable soil of the rocky mountainside as they had for hundreds, perhaps even thousands, of years.

Jason paused at a blue-painted door set in a high wall, which was freshly white in marked contrast to its dingy neighbors. The door opened easily, swinging on oiled hinges, and he gestured to Sophie to precede him. The doorway was so low that he had to duck his head to avoid banging it on the lintel.

Inside, a paved terrace was furnished with a plain wooden table and the ubiquitous rush-seated straight chairs, while around them painted pots held a profusion of brightly colored flowers. A grapevine laden with clusters of purple-black fruit partially shaded the terrace, the shadows of the leaves outlined in stark relief against the snowy wall of the low house.

Jason rapped sharply on the door, and after a moment it creaked open an inch or two. A pair of bright, birdlike eyes in a face whose skin was creased into a network of fine wrinkles regarded them with suspicion that miraculously changed to joy as the tiny, bent old woman threw the door wide and enfolded Jason in an affectionate embrace.

"Jason," she cried happily, "you've come to see me."

"How have you been, Aunt Maria?" He gently extricated himself from his aunt's arms, kissing her cheek as he did so, and took Sophie's hand. "I've brought my wife Sophie to meet you."

The bright black eyes regarded Sophie with disconcerting shrewdness, then the old lady nodded, apparently liking what she saw. Sophie was irresistibly reminded of her own grandmother, whom she had met only once when she was five on the occasion of that lady's visit to her son in Canada. Small as she had been, Sophie had never forgotten. Her grandmother had died not long after.

Sophie bent her head and kissed Aunt Maria's wrinkled cheek, which had the softness of a well-washed chamois and smelled of lavender cologne. Perhaps this, most of all, recalled her grandmother.

To Jason Aunt Maria said, "You're a lucky man. She's beautiful. A bit thin, but then that seems to be the fashion nowadays."

The interior of the little house was plain but scrupulously clean, the ceilings so low that Jason could barely stand upright. The only luxury in evidence was a large television set, which occupied the place of honor in the corner of the room.

"You must stay to lunch," Aunt Maria urged them, and Sophie was inordinately pleased when Jason consented. His aunt insisted she had plenty for them to eat, but Jason said that since it was a festive occasion, he would go out and get a bottle of wine.

Left alone with Sophie, the old woman fingered the fabric of Sophie's dress. "Lovely material," she said. She sighed deeply. "My daughters live in Australia now, but when they come to visit they have dresses like that."

Sophie was amused to realize that the aunt thought her dress to be of foreign manufacture when in reality she had purchased it in Athens, but she didn't have the heart to correct her. "May I help you with something?" she asked somewhat shyly.

"No, no, you'll ruin your pretty dress."

"But I'd like to help," Sophie insisted.

Aunt Maria sighed and took a folded tablecloth from a drawer. Sophie smoothed the fine linen on the table. "This linen. It's so fine. I've never seen anything like it. Is it made locally?"

Aunt Maria smiled. "No, I have a cousin in Crete. It's made there in a convent."

Sophie's mind was racing. If she did open a shop in Athens, this would sell very well, Even modern Greek brides bought linens for their hope chests, and the quality of this was the best she'd seen. It could even be made into dresses.

Jason came back, bringing not only wine but a bottle of a sweet liqueur that Sophie had tasted and disliked intensely but that she knew Aunt Maria would appreciate.

They ate the simple meal with enjoyment, later talking far into the afternoon. As the lowering sun began to slant through the narrow, lace-curtained windows, Aunt Maria prevailed upon them to spend the night. Sophie was somewhat surprised when Jason readily accepted the invitation, wondering where they would sleep in the small house.

She was pleasantly enlightened when his aunt opened one of the two doors at the end of the room, revealing a spartan chamber furnished with a brass bed. The room smelled strongly of mothballs, but this soon dissipated when the windows were opened wide to receive the fresh evening breeze that swept off the mountain slopes. The other door concealed a surprisingly modern bathroom, in what appeared to be a much later addition to the old cottage.

While Jason was out getting their luggage from the car, which had to remain in the square, Aunt Maria talked about him, revealing his earlier background that had so strongly influenced his character. It was obvious that his aunt doted on him, but Sophie had no doubt that she spoke only the truth.

"Jason bought the television for me," Aunt Maria told her. "And he had the bathroom built. It was quite a change, I can tell you," she added, laughing merrily, "from going outside in the middle of the night and freezing in an outdoor shower in winter."

Sophie was touched that Jason had concerned himself with his relatives after he had become a success in life. So many rich men left families and forgot them as they climbed the ladder of financial success.

"How can you stay in this village when there are so few other people?" Sophie asked. "I'm sure you could come and live with us in Athens." She hardly noticed that she used the collective pronoun, as though the continuance of her marriage were a foregone conclusion.

"Jason has asked me many times," Aunt Maria said. "But I couldn't live in a city. I'm like those olive trees out there. My roots are in this stony ground, and I would die if I tried to tear them up."

Later, lying in the brass bed next to Jason, Sophie listened to the silence. How peaceful it was with only the wind sighing through the olive leaves, whispering secret messages to the crickets, which answered with their rhythmic chirring. The moon cast a radiance on the bed, washing the room in its cool white light.

The night was hot and they lay uncovered, their bodies barely touching. Sophie could see Jason's eyes gleaming in the semidarkness as he lay on his side watching her, his hand lying possessively on her bare thigh.

"Jason, I'm glad you brought me here." Her voice was a whisper. She didn't want to disturb Aunt Maria sleeping in the main room of the cottage. "Why did you never bring me before?"

"I don't know," he said softly. "There didn't seem to be time. Anyway, I thought you might be shocked. It's a very poor place."

Sophie was hurt that he had thought her so shallow that she would look down on these people merely because they lacked material possessions. Their spirit and independence made them rich. "Poverty isn't a crime," she said with a touch of asperity.

"There are some who think it is," Jason replied with faint irony. "Shaw said it was the worst of crimes."

Sophie sighed, refusing to let him draw her into an argument and disrupt the peaceful night with conflict.

"I'm not shocked to see this place. Besides, you've done a lot for your aunt. Probably for others as well."

He did not deny this. "I've tried. But these people are proud and independent. It's difficult to help them. I paid for the school in the next village so that the children could be educated in a modern facility in their own village, hoping they will stay and not let these remote areas die out entirely." He said this matter-of-factly, in no way flaunting his ability to buy what the residents themselves found beyond their means. "The village, of course, does not know where the money came from," he added. "But they could not refuse an anonymous donation."

Sophie felt a surge of warmth toward him such as she had never before experienced. He wasn't as callous and uncaring as she had thought him, and the idea moved her to speculate that perhaps she had misjudged him in other matters as well.

His hand moved almost imperceptibly up her thigh to her hip, then trailed across the flat of her stomach.

"Jason, don't!" she hissed. "Your aunt!" But she was powerless to move away from his sensuous touch, and in any case she couldn't have gone far in the narrow confines of the bed.

Jason's mouth touched hers with a series of feather-light kisses that had her groaning inaudibly for more. "What about my aunt?" he whispered. "She's asleep."

"But it's her house," Sophie persisted, quivering under his hands that were stroking her small, pert breasts.

"So?" She could see the amused lifting of his eyebrows. "Do you think she got her children from under a cabbage plant? Or perhaps the stork that nests on the bell tower brought them?"

Sophie shook her head. "But I don't want to tonight."

Jason laughed softly, the purr of a cat who has eaten the cream and wants the canary as well. His breath was warm and toothpaste-scented, sweet against her mouth. "Of course you want to, Sophie. Tonight and every other night." He grasped her face with his long fingers, compelling her to meet his eyes. "Don't you?"

Chagrined to admit to the fire lapping at her nerve endings, she tried to evade his hand. He lowered his head, and his mouth possessed hers, making an insistent exploration that caused her to moan with pleasure. He began to love her with slow, sensuous movements of his hands and body until she wanted to scream for release from the tension inside her. With his uncanny perception and intimate knowledge of her body, he covered her mouth with his and stifled the cry that arose in her as the tension exploded in a paroxysm of delight that started tears streaming from her eyes.

Jason held her in his arms, kissing the tears away with great tenderness as though now that he had won—had successfully coerced her into an overwhelming response—he could be generous. Sophie thought hopelessly, *Is he going to go on punishing me?*

Then she could almost feel she had imagined it as he began to talk, his voice barely above a whisper. She listened, knowing he might never again let her into the room in his mind that contained his past and the hardships he would never be able to forget.

"My mother came from one of the leading families of the next village, the one where I paid for the school. Her father wished her to marry a man whose family had the large house at the end of this street, which we passed this afternoon.'' Sophie remembered the house, once magnificent but now falling into ruin.

"This family owned a good many of the olive trees you see on the mountain,'' he went on. "As did my grandfather. He had flocks of sheep and goats as well, and my mother occasionally helped to care for them, taking them to pasture. One day in the hills she met my father, also caring for sheep, and they fell in love. Her father would not hear of her marrying a poor man, however. It would better his fortunes, as well as his standing in the village, if she married the rich man. Besides, in those days, arrangements of this sort were not broken off lightly.''

"Did a feud start between the families?'' Sophie asked sleepily.

She could feel Jason shaking with laughter. "No, my sweet, nothing so romantic. Actually there haven't been any feuds here for over sixty years. The tower isn't used except by children playing bandits. No, they did the obvious thing. Met secretly until it was apparent that she was pregnant. The father of the rich man immediately called off the arrangement, and my grandfather, to save the family reputation, hastily got the priest to marry her to the man she loved.''

Sophie digested this in silence, sinking deeper into drowsiness. She had nearly dropped off when Jason spoke again. "Does it shock you that I came within a few months of being a bastard?''

"No,'' she murmured. "They loved each other. I know, because your father told me how happy they were together.''

"Yes,'' Jason whispered. "I was a love child, and I was always the wild one.'' He turned his head and kissed her softly parted mouth. "Good night, Sophie." But she was too far gone into slumber to answer.

In the morning there was fresh goat's milk for breakfast, which Sophie found she enjoyed despite the initial strangeness of the taste. She had a brief thought that it would be wonderful to live this simple life, close to nature. But at the same time she knew that no one can go back to his past; circumstances change, and, most of all, people change.

Aunt Maria walked with them to the square, bidding them a tearful farewell. As the Jaguar reached the bend in the rough road, Sophie looked back and waved to the lonely figure standing forlornly against the backdrop of the empty, dilapidated houses, wondering if she would ever see the old lady again.

Jason wished to reach Athens that same day and drove steadily by the most direct route, through Gythion and then north. He had retreated into a shell of his own making, which Sophie dared not attempt to penetrate. After a few tentative remarks failed to produce other than monosyllabic responses, she lapsed into silence. The nearer they approached Athens, the more melancholy Jason became, as though he too sensed that this trip had been less decisive than they had hoped, that the future was still by no means clear.

Part of Sophie longed to reassure him, to passionately declare that she would stay with him; but the other, less optimistic part of her, reinforced in its doubts by his moodiness, cautiously refused to believe that his basic attitude toward her had changed.

Ten

They arrived late in the evening, finding the house largely in darkness. Leaving the suitcases in the hall to be taken up later, Jason led Sophie into the living room where several lamps still glowed. As they entered, a tall, slender figure uncoiled itself from a deep armchair. Sophie felt the blood drain from her face, but the other two seemed to have eyes only for each other.

"Helen, how nice to see you," Jason exclaimed, taking his cousin by the upper arms and kissing both her cheeks. Helen adroitly managed to turn her face and receive one of the kisses on her full red lips, leaving a smear of lipstick at the corner of Jason's mouth.

"I thought I'd surprise you," she trilled in a markedly American accent. "And little Sophie is here, too." This in a deceptively sweet tone that set Sophie's teeth on edge. This woman had been at least indirectly the cause of the breakup between her and Jason, and she had hoped never to see her again.

They exchanged pleasantries, which to Sophie's sensitized hearing were at times slightly barbed. Jason moved to the other side of the room to pour wine for the two women, and Sophie said softly so that he could not hear, "Helen, what do you want?"

The other woman's cold, beautiful face wore a malicious smile. "Why, I heard you were here, so I thought I'd come and see how you and Jason were getting along."

"As you see, we're getting along," Sophie retorted. "So you can leave. We don't need you."

Helen regarded her steadily for a moment, her eyes narrowing. "Well, well," she sneered. "The kitten has sprouted claws. It's Jason's house, and I've always been welcome to stay as long as I like."

"It's my house, too," Sophie blurted furiously. "I'm his wife."

From the corner of her eye she saw Jason approaching with the drinks. Helen, however, managed to get in the last word. "We'll see, darling." She leaned forward so that only Sophie could hear. "Does Jason know about the baby?"

Sophie felt suddenly chilled to the bone, and afraid, but fortunately Jason was looking at Helen and seemed not to notice. She had to accept the glass from his hand, but she could not conceal the haste with which she consumed the contents. Saying she had a headache from the long drive, which brought an apparently sympathetic look from Helen—whom Jason was watching—she escaped from the room, hoping that Jason would soon follow before Helen did irreparable damage to the fragile repairs in their relationship.

Her worst fears were soon realized. She had showered and was seated at her dressing table in her lace-trimmed negligee brushing her hair when he burst into the room, throwing open the door with such force that it slammed against the wall, knocking a piece of plaster to the floor. He glared for an instant at the wall, then kicked the door shut as if punishing it for the damage.

Sophie shrank back before the raging flames that shot from his eyes, while at the same time a detached portion of her mind hoped that Stavros was a sound sleeper and would be spared what she feared was the final battle of the war between them. With a strange fatalism, she knew what was coming and she had no defenses.

Jason advanced to the center of the room and stood glaring at her, his fists clenching and unclenching at his sides as though he wished they were around her neck.

"What kind of woman are you?" he said at last in a low, deadly voice. "How could you hate me that much?"

"Jason," Sophie cried, her hands reaching out to him in helpless supplication.

"She told me you killed it." His voice was strangled, as though he could hardly get out the words.

"I didn't," Sophie insisted, fighting for her life. "It was an accident."

Jason's eyes were opaque, as though he were seeing something too awful to contemplate. Sophie had a feeling he was not seeing her at all. He sank down on the edge of the bed, his face buried in his hands. "Sophie, did you hate me so much that you couldn't bear to have my child? Our baby should be playing in the sunshine—won't he be crying in your dreams forever?"

"Jason, he already does," Sophie said gently. "Why do you think I have those nightmares? They started after I lost the baby."

"Then why, Sophie?" He sounded tired, completely without hope, his voice muffled by his hands.

"I would have given anything for it not to have happened. You must believe that."

"Then why did it happen? Why did you make that choice? Sophie, just tell me that."

"It was not my choice," Sophie said desperately. "I fell on the icy steps and had a miscarriage." She added in a voice torn with anguish, "It was a boy."

Jason raised his head and looked at her. Sophie shuddered at the loathing in his eyes. "Don't lie to me, Sophie. Helen says you threw yourself down the steps deliberately, that you said you would get rid of the child one way or another."

So Helen knew the circumstances—either her friends, or even Sophie's father in all innocence, might have described the accident—but she had twisted them in a diabolical way that Sophie could not think how to fight. A numbness invaded her brain as she saw the extent to which Helen would go to get what she wanted—namely, Jason. How clever she had been, biding her time until the right psychological moment when the disclosure would have the maximum effect. And Jason believed her.

Sophie, even in her extremity, could find some excuse for him. Helen was his cousin, however distant, and he had never had a reason to doubt her word. Sophie had no doubt that she had imparted the information to him in such a way that no mud would fall on Helen. Perhaps

Helen had even expressed sympathy for poor, mixed-up Sophie, so young to be facing having a child alone.

All the blood in her body turned to ice. "If that's what she said and you believe it, that's all I have to say," she said with cold dignity. "If you don't mind, I'd like to go to bed now."

Jason stood up, swaying slightly with reaction. He walked to the door like a sleepwalker meticulously treading the top edge of a very high wall. Sophie was alarmed in spite of her cold anger.

She stood for a moment in indecision, then opened the door he had closed after him and silently descended the stairs. He was in the living room, where to her relief Helen was not in evidence. He stood at the sideboard, a large bottle of *ouzo* held to his lips, his throat moving rhythmically as he drank it down steadily as if it were no stronger than water.

"Jason," Sophie said. But her voice would not rise above a horrified whisper.

He put down the empty bottle with exaggerated care and went past her, seeming not to see her in the doorway.

She heard the front door closing, its faint click somehow more terrible than a bang. The Jaguar's engine leaped to life with its distinctive roar, and she flung open the door, running down the steps as he turned the car in the driveway. The headlights swung around and caught her in their beam, but he did not hesitate. He gunned the motor and swept down the drive, so close to her that she felt the wind of his passage. With a deafening screech of tortured tires, he turned into the street and raced away.

Sophie sank to her knees in the sharp gravel of the driveway, sobbing with fear. "Oh, God," she implored, gazing up at the stars overhead, "don't let him be killed."

After a long time she picked herself up and somehow made it back to the bedroom where she lay dry-eyed and sleepless until morning, unable even to cry.

Going downstairs when she heard by the sounds in the kitchen that the household was awake, she was surprised to find Paul in the hall on his way up. Before she could frame a question, he spoke. "Jason phoned from the office. He wants me to take him a change of clothes." He looked closely at Sophie's haggard appearance, which even skillful makeup could not disguise. "Say, what happened between you two?"

Sophie shook her head, pushing her loose hair back from her forehead with one hand. "I can't tell you, Paul," she said wretchedly. "Did Jason sound all right?"

"Well," Paul answered, giving her a speculative look out of narrowed eyes, "he sounded like you look. Say, Sophie, I'll tell him to come home early. Maybe you can make up."

"I doubt it, Paul," said Sophie. "Shall I pack the clothes? What did he say he wanted?"

"His gray suit, and a shirt and tie to go with it. I'll be here when you bring it down. There should be an overnight bag for the small items."

"Yes, I know where it is." Sophie turned and went back up the stairs. She selected a shirt and tie and packed them in the case, then as an afterthought added a change of underwear—Jason liked to be fresh from the skin out every day. She fought back tears as she carried the case and the suit down to the waiting Paul.

He subjected her to a long, searching gaze but made no comment on the evidence of tears quivering on her lashes. "Thanks, Sophie. See you later."

Sophie went into the kitchen where Voula was putting a batch of the sweet rolls Stavros liked into the oven. She looked up in surprise as Sophie came in. "My, everyone is up early this morning."

"I haven't been to bed," Sophie said baldly.

Voula's dark eyes regarded her narrowly. "And you look it, too," she said bluntly. She made a gesture with her head, indicating the upper regions of the house. "I knew as soon as she came back that that woman would be trouble."

"So you heard all the noise."

Voula rolled her eyes expressively. "Who wouldn't have? Fortunately, Stavros took a sleeping pill last night since he didn't feel very well. He seems to have slept through the whole thing."

Sophie sank down on a chair, covering her face with trembling hands. "What shall I do?" she whispered in a small, hopeless voice.

"Nothing until Jason comes home, as he's bound to some time today," Voula said practically. "Perhaps he'll have cooled off. What was it all about, anyway? Jason and Helen were talking in the study, though I couldn't hear what was said when I brought the coffee things from the living room. The next thing I knew, he was storming upstairs."

Sophie lifted her head, her gray eyes the only color in her ashen face. "He thinks I got rid of his baby," she said starkly.

Voula knelt down and took Sophie in her arms. "Oh, Sophie. How could he think that of you?"

"Helen told him I had, and he believed her. But I didn't," she cried wildly. "I slipped on the icy steps when I went out that morning to pick up Father's paper. I hit my head, and the next thing I knew I was in the hospital, and I'd lost the baby. Our little boy." Her voice cracked, and she broke into uncontrolled sobbing.

Voula held her, patting her back, letting her cry. It was not only the sleepless night but all the remembered anguish over the loss of the child that came flooding back. She had lost both Jason and his son, who would have been the only part of him she had left. Her father had tried in every way to comfort her, but she had moved through each day for weeks like a victim of shell shock. Only when her father's health had begun to fail again had she pulled herself together and returned to the land of the living.

Voula was murmuring soothingly. "There, there, Sophie, cry it all out. You'll feel better."

Gradually the sobs subsided to an occasional hiccup, and Sophie groped for a handkerchief. Voula delved into her apron pocket, bringing out her own, immaculately pressed and smelling of eau de cologne. Sophie mopped up, composing herself although her face remained deathly pale.

"Voula, you said that Jason drank after I left." Sophie's voice was hoarse but steady. "Were there also other women? No, don't look like that. I can take it. I want the truth."

Voula hesitated, casting her mind back over the intervening two years. "At first he drank as I told you, but then the business went through some kind of crisis and he buried himself in his work. Why? Did you think there were?"

"Helen told me that all of Athens was talking about how much Jason was neglecting his wife to take out other women."

Voula piously crossed herself. "That woman must be the devil incarnate."

"But Jason can't see that," Sophie said dryly.

"She is, after all, his cousin," Voula admitted. "They've known each other all their lives. They even lived together when the family came to Athens. Family feeling is strong."

"Voula, do you remember when I left before? Helen was in Athens at the time. Was she here much after I left?"

Voula, seeing the tension on Sophie's face as she voiced this question, knew it was not being asked lightly. Her brow furrowed as she strove to remember the exact day and order of events. Her face cleared. "No, she wasn't here at all. She went to Jamaica where her ex-husband had fallen ill while on holiday. He died soon after, and she spent months in New York clearing up his affairs. I doubt that she went to him out of real concern, but her show of feeling paid off when he left her the bulk of his estate."

Sophie said thoughtfully, "How long was Jason in New York at that time?"

"Only a few days. He didn't take any more trips for several months after that one. That was the time he was drinking so much."

"So Jason didn't see her for months after I left," Sophie mused, half to herself. She was appalled at the duplicity of the woman in boldly lying to her. Mixed with this was anger at herself for being fool enough to believe the lies.

"He might have seen her sometime, but for at least six months he was here and she was there, with an ocean between them," Voula stated with conviction. "Did you think there was something between them?"

"It doesn't matter now. It's too late."

"Sophie." Voula laid a hand gently on the younger woman's shoulder. "I'm sure Jason never thought of Helen that way. I've seen them together many times, and he treats her like a sister."

"Yes," said Sophie absently, thinking that Helen certainly didn't see Jason as a brother.

There was a short silence during which Voula began to take the pans of fragrant rolls out of the oven, transferring them to a wicker basket.

"Voula, why is Helen staying here now? She has her own apartment, hasn't she?"

Voula lifted her shoulders in an eloquent shrug. "She arrived yesterday afternoon, saying her apartment is being redecorated and asking if she could stay here for a few days. Of course Stavros said yes."

She handed the basket of rolls to Sophie. "Would you take these out? Stavros will be waiting for his breakfast."

The old man, looking dear and familiar to Sophie's eyes, was already out on the terrace, reading his morning paper. She put down the basket and kissed him tenderly. He smiled at her, the smile fading as he examined her more closely. "I thought the holiday would do you good, but you look worse than ever."

Slightly put out by his disconcerting honesty, Sophie nevertheless summoned a brave smile, saying, "I didn't sleep well last night."

Stavros looked at the place settings on the table. "Where are the boys this morning?"

"They've already gone out," Voula put in. "And knowing Helen, she won't be down for some hours yet. She never has breakfast."

In Stavros' undemanding presence, Sophie threw off some of her depression. When Jason came home she would talk to him, try to convince him that she was not responsible for losing their baby. If he was willing to accept her explanation, perhaps there was a chance that they could yet salvage their marriage from the wreckage. Her face became grim as she considered how Helen had deliberately set out to break them up. And gullible Sophie had eagerly swallowed every lie, playing right into her hands. She made up her mind that she would have a few words with Helen the moment she put in an appearance.

After breakfast, Stavros, blissfully unaware that this might well be Sophie's last day, called a taxi and went to spend the day with his bedridden friend. Sophie purposely hung around the living room, waiting for Helen to come down.

She appeared just before lunch, dressed for town.

"Helen," Sophie called from the living room. "I'd like a word with you, please."

Helen advanced warily into the room, her cold eyes narrowing as she noted the resolution in the set of Sophie's chin. "Can you make it fast, darling," she drawled. "I'm meeting someone for lunch."

"Are you?" Sophie queried in a hard voice that was not at all like her own. "Well, you can take a few minutes to pack your suitcase and take it with you. I don't want you here interfering with our lives any more."

"You can't make me go," Helen stated, turning toward the door as if she had decided the interview was at an end.

"Wait," Sophie said sharply. "I'm not through yet. Why did you lie two years ago, and tell me you were having an affair with Jason? Voula told me that you couldn't have at the time you mentioned."

"Are you sure I lied?" Helen asked brazenly. "You know Voula would tell you anything she thought you'd want to hear. Besides, you were quick enough to believe me."

"Voula wouldn't lie," Sophie retorted, holding on to her temper with difficulty.

Helen shrugged. "It makes no difference. Jason is finished with you now, and I have the upper hand. You never understood him the way I do. Only someone who saw him come up from squalor to this success could understand. You wanted him to leave his work and play with you. You never understood his need never to be poor again. If you'd trusted him, Sophie, and allowed him to be himself, you could have kept him so easily."

Sophie paled; she heard the truth in the accusation and was deeply ashamed.

Helen, seeing her pallor, smirked in self-satisfaction. "I'm sure Jason would be interested in all the men you went out with in Vancouver after you left him."

"That's an outright lie," Sophie cried. "Jason would never believe that."

Helen's delicate brows lifted in mocking derision. "Wouldn't he? I had no trouble convincing him about the baby."

Sophie felt faint, all the fight draining out of her. Jason was shrewd about people, hardly a man to allow anyone to pull the wool over his eyes. But Helen could tell the most convincing lies without turning a hair, and he might well believe her again, especially when the lie concerned something that aroused his jealousy. Since his opinion of Sophie had already hit rock bottom, another story would only reinforce his contempt.

"Get out," Sophie hissed through white lips. "Get out before I break a lamp over your head."

Head held high, Helen walked out, her high heels clicking on the tiled hall floor. Sophie only stirred when Voula poked her head around the corner and asked if she wanted lunch.

"No, thank you, Voula. I have a headache. I'm going to lie down."

"That might be best," Voula agreed. "That woman is enough to give anyone a headache. When Jason comes home, you can have a talk with him."

Not if Helen gets to him first, Sophie thought in despair.

Eleven

———

Sophie slept for a time, waking unrefreshed. Downstairs she found to her surprise that Paul had returned. "Paul," she said, "could I speak to you for a moment?"

"Certainly. In Jason's study?"

They went in and he closed the door. "What is it, Sophie?"

She gave him a brief outline of what had occurred, glossing over the details. "I have to leave," she said at the end. "Jason and I talked about it the other day. I have to see to the shop. I'll try to get a flight out tomorrow."

Paul frowned. "Shouldn't you talk to Jason first?"

"I want to, but I'm afraid he's not going to listen to me. He's never going to believe me in the face of Helen's lies."

Paul considered, his boyish face serious. "I'll help you, Sophie, but I still think it would be better for you to stay and fight. Running away never solves anything; it only puts it off. I'm sure once he gets over his shock about the baby, Jason will listen to you.''

"You didn't see how he was last night." Sophie shook her head, losing her composure for a moment. She took a deep breath to steady her jumping nerves. "He was like a crazy man. He drank a whole bottle of *ouzo*."

Paul let out a long whistle. "For someone who rarely drinks, he can certainly put it away when he wants to."

"It's not funny, Paul," Sophie said indignantly. "And he drove the car afterward. He could have been killed."

"I'm not laughing, Sophie." Paul came over and put his arm about her shoulders. "Actually, I gave Stavros some *ouzo* yesterday afternoon. If it was the same bottle, it was only a little over half full. Still, that's a good amount to drink at one time." He paused reflectively. "No wonder Jason looked like something the cat dragged in this morning."

He squeezed her shoulders. "Try not to worry too much. Actually, on second thought, if you go away maybe Jason will come to his senses and go after you."

"I doubt it, Paul. He didn't last time. And even if he does, I'm not sure I want a husband who so easily takes someone else's word over that of his wife. He has no faith in me."

"Did you have faith in him?" Paul countered with a perception that prompted her to wonder if perhaps she had misjudged the depth of his character. "From what I gather, you thought he was fooling around, and that's one reason you left him. Did you ever ask him about that?"

"I did," Sophie insisted. "But he wouldn't talk about it. Then Helen told me what she did, and I had no reason to doubt it. Everyone was talking about him."

"Still, you might have heard Jason's side. There are
women in business, you know, and Jason would have
had to deal with them on occasion, even on a social level.
You mustn't believe all the gossip that was going around
about him."

"I know," Sophie said wearily. "But it's too late
now." It was becoming a refrain, ringing in her head:
Too late, too late. She covered her face with her hands,
crying in quiet hopelessness, the tears running between
her fingers. Paul put his arms around her and held her
close to him. Needing the physical comfort of nearness
to another human being, she buried her face against his
shoulder.

At that moment the door opened, and Jason walked
in. Sophie lifted her head, and, seeing his face, her heart
turned to ice.

"Keep your hands off my wife," he thundered, his
face savage as she had never seen it.

"Your wife," sneered Paul, recovering from his initial dismay with remarkable swiftness. He put Sophie
gently to one side. "Then have the decency to treat her
like a wife. Have a little faith in her."

"What do you mean, faith?" Jason said belliger-
ently. "I come in here and find her in your arms, and you
have the nerve to talk about faith. I ought to kill you
both."

"Jason, listen to me," Paul said desperately, inching
back under the fierce heat of Jason's anger until he came
up against the desk.

Sophie stood helplessly by, not knowing what she
could do to stop them. The sight of the two of them savagely glaring at each other with electricity crackling between them, like two stallions about to engage in battle

over a harem of mares, sickened her to her very bones. She tried to impose herself between them, but in the heat of their animosity, she might have been invisible for all the attention they paid her.

Jason, reviving dormant skills learned in the rough-and-tumble of the Athens streets, got in the first blow, but Paul was not far behind. Spurred on by the knowledge of being in the right and in defense of a woman, he made up in enthusiasm for what he lacked in skill. He landed his fist more accurately than Jason had, causing blood to spurt from Jason's nose, startling crimson on his white shirt. This only served to enrage Jason further, and he swung viciously, connecting with Paul's cheekbone. Paul, smaller and lighter than his brother, paled with obvious pain and almost fell.

Sophie had had enough. "Stop it," she screamed. "Stop it, both of you." They paused, startled, staring at her as if she had suddenly grown horns. "Stop it," she repeated more quietly. "You're behaving like animals, and I refuse to have anything more to do with either of you. I'm going, and you can kill each other for all I care." She turned and marched out of the room, leaving them gazing after her in openmouthed amazement.

Up in her room she washed her face and was drying it when Jason burst unannounced into the bathroom. His shirt was a mess and stripping it off, he dumped it into the wastebasket.

Sophie made an unnecessary little business of hanging up the towel, arranging it on the bar so that it was absolutely straight. She turned to find Jason regarding his gory appearance in the mirror, his expression wry and, she thought disgustedly, touched with a kind of sheepish pride. The muscles under the supple skin of his shoulders rippled like gold silk as he turned on the tap. She could see the heavy mat of hair covering his broad chest and narrow, flat stomach, and her fingers tingled as, in spite of everything, she was seized with a sudden longing to touch him.

His dark blue eyes met hers in the glass. "Well, Sophie?" he asked sardonically. The hostility seemed largely to have left him, erased no doubt by the fight.

She licked her dry lips. "Nothing was going on between Paul and me, but of course you couldn't wait for an explanation."

His gaze did not waver. After a small pause he said, "You must realize how it looked."

Sophie turned away wearily. "Oh, Jason, you always think you're the only one who is right. You don't believe me about the baby. I can't live with your lack of faith anymore. I'm leaving tomorrow, as soon as I can get a seat on an airplane."

For an instant he looked startled, then the cold mask fell over his features. "As you wish." He stopped and swallowed hard before adding, the mask slipping, "But you'll be back?" It was as if he forced himself to ask, but did not expect anything but a negative answer.

Sophie said, "Not as long as Helen is welcome in this house, and maybe never. You must be blind, Jason, that you can't see her for what she is."

"But Helen is my cousin." Some of the tautness of anger was returning. "What could she possibly have to gain by lying about you?"

"Why don't you ask her? If you want to take Helen's word over mine, Jason, that's your prerogative, but I know she's lied to me. So think about it. Maybe she's also lied to you." With that, she walked out of the room.

When Sophie awoke the next morning, there was no one in the bed with her and no sign that Jason had slept there. Her mind made up after a night of much soul-searching and little sleep, she showered and dressed in clothes suitable for traveling. Quickly and efficiently she packed her suitcase and smaller carryon bag. Her mind went back over the previous evening. Jason hadn't shown up for dinner, nor had he appeared later, thus preventing her from talking to him. Whether or not he'd avoided her on purpose, she didn't know. Helen had sat at the table as if nothing had happened, and that for Sophie had been the final indignity.

She snapped her cases shut. Now for the most difficult task of all, taking leave of Stavros.

The house was uncannily quiet. Where was everyone? The large clock in the hall began to toll the hour, and she paused, counting the sonorous notes. Eleven. She looked at her watch. Seven-twenty. It had stopped. No wonder the house was quiet. The men had gone to their offices. Helen's whereabouts never even occurred to her. It was as though in her mind the woman who had shattered her life no longer existed.

She found Stavros on the terrace, drinking his morning coffee.

"Well, Sophie, how are you?" Then as he took in her appearance, the trim linen suit she was wearing, he added, "Are you going out?"

"I'm leaving," she said as gently as possible.

His bristly brows lifted slightly, but his surprise was less marked than she would have expected. "Oh? I'm sorry. Will Jason be going later to join you?"

She spread her hands in a helpless gesture. "I don't know."

Stavros said, after a brief pause, "I hope Jason will be home tonight."

"Why? Has he suddenly gone on a business trip?" Come to think of it, where had Jason slept?

"No," Stavros said. "There was an accident at one of our factories near Mandra. They telephoned last night not long after dinner."

"Serious?" Sophie asked, concerned.

Stavros shook his head. "Not as bad as it could have been. Several men were injured, but only one seriously. He'll recover. But the whole incident must be investigated, and Jason's been out all night, over there."

So Jason had not spent the night with Helen. Sophie drew scant consolation from the knowledge.

"Have you arranged your flight?" Stavros asked.

"No, but my return ticket is still valid. I won't have any trouble. I'll stay at a hotel near the airport if I can't get a seat today. Paul's taking care of the rented car."

"Why don't you stay here, Sophie?"

Sophie twisted her fingers together uncomfortably, her gaze dropping to the toes of her neat tan pumps. "I'd rather not see Jason again just now." Seeing Stavros' questioning look, she added, "He knows I'm leaving."

A lump of tears threatened to choke her, and she quickly bent and kissed the dear old man's leathery cheek. "Good-bye, *Patera*. You've been a wonderful friend."

Stavros kissed her back with tenderness and affection. "Try not to worry too much. Jason will realize what he's throwing away, and come and get you."

Hearing his kind words, the tears almost overflowed, and she averted her face. "Excuse me, I have to say good-bye to Voula."

Voula was in the kitchen and expressed no surprise that Sophie was leaving. "That Jason needs his head examined," she said succinctly.

Sophie sighed. "We probably were just not meant for each other. Good-bye, Voula."

Voula hugged her warmly. "Good-bye, Sophie." She added the traditional Greek farewell. "Be happy."

Stavros accompanied Sophie out to the taxi waiting in the driveway. He kissed her again before handing her into the vehicle. "Remember, you can always call on us if there is anything you need."

Tears were trickling down Sophie's cheeks. "Good-bye, *Patera*. I'll write to you."

She saw him through a mist of tears as the taxi moved away, an old man standing before the beautiful and luxurious rich man's house. How trivial possessions were if there were no happiness in the house.

It was still dark when Sophie presented herself at the airlines terminal the next morning. The line was long, adults dull-eyed with sleep, the children bright and excited, clutching dolls or teddy bears. Ahead of her, a little boy regarded her over his mother's shoulder, his eyes round and unblinking, dark and fringed by extravagantly long lashes. She felt a sharp pang for the child she had lost. If only Jason had been understanding, willing to listen. She would have been able to exorcise the faint guilt she had always felt. If only she hadn't gone out that morning, the morning it was icy. If only.

She received her boarding pass, then joined the line at passport control. The passengers were herded into the little shuttle bus and driven to the other end of the field.

An unpromising gray dawn covered the heavy sky, and Sophie could see the giant plane waiting, its powerful engines muttering, warming up. A wicked wind, harbinger of autumn, whipped across the open field off the sea, tugging boldly at her skirt, loosening strands of her pale hair from its confining knot and blowing them untidily about her face, which was pinched with cold and misery.

She settled gratefully into the warm cocoon of the airplane, closing her eyes wearily. She only looked down when the plane was airborne, staring bleakly at the little twinkling lights of the city through gaps in the heavy overcast. Then they were above the clouds and bound for London.

Sophie landed in Vancouver to brilliant sunshine and a summerlike warmth. Outside the terminal, as she lined up for a taxi, the sun momentarily blinded her. Tired as she was, she couldn't help but notice little details—the enormous cars—a Mercedes looked tiny—and the smallness of the license plates, less than half the size of those in Greece. She also noticed the tense, hurried look of the people, and in the line, the stolid, orderly waiting, no pushing to be first. A wave of loneliness swept over her as she watched families reuniting, the hugs and kisses.

The next morning, Sophie went to the shop. Laura greeted her exuberantly, a tall young woman with masses of dark hair, a bright vivacious face and the lean body of a model. After kissing her, she held Sophie at arms' length and searched her face. "You're browner, but otherwise the trip didn't improve your looks at all," she stated bluntly. "What happened?"

She led Sophie into the back room and began to make coffee as Sophie related the events that had occurred. "You should have stayed and fought for him."

She might have been able to fight Helen, if she'd had to, Sophie thought dismally. Jason's contempt she could not.

"How could I, when Jason wouldn't even listen?" she said. "Anyway, he knew I was planning to come back for the shop." Sophie added sugar to the mug of coffee Laura set before her, stirring the creamy liquid so furiously it slopped onto the desk. "If he wants me back, he'll have to come after me."

"Like he did last time?" Laura asked.

"If he ever did, it might prove something," Sophie said flatly.

"It might at that," Laura agreed. Her frown lifted. "Anyway, with the new stock coming in, the shop will be busy enough to keep both of us occupied." She turned to go to the front of the shop as the bell over the door announced their first customer of the day.

Sophie, while grateful for Laura's concern, was relieved to see her go. Her emotions were still too raw to make it easy for her to discuss them. She needed time for scars to form again around her heart.

She pulled the ledger toward her and began to look over the accounts, wishing she could regain her erstwhile enthusiasm for her work. But since seeing Jason again, even that didn't fill the void in her. So much for ambition.

Twelve

———

In her apartment that evening, Sophie stared out at the rain washing down the windowpane. Yesterday's sunshine certainly hadn't lasted long.

She moved away from the window, twitching the curtain back into place, her depression deepening. She turned on the television. Several cars were demolished before her eyes with their drivers emerging unhurt. Pure fantasy. With a grimace, she switched channels and finally settled on a talk show. After it ended, a gory thriller was displaying its opening titles, dripping with blood, when the doorbell rang, startling her so that her heart began to pound. She turned off the television and went to the door.

"Open up," said a voice with unmistakable authority.

Sophie pressed a trembling hand to her mouth, her head reeling dizzily. It couldn't be. Weariness of body and spirit must be making her hallucinate. The voice came again. "Sophie, I know you're in there. Open the door, please."

Slowly she released the lock and pulled the door open. Jason stood there, carrying a suitcase, his face unshaven and haggard. Raindrops sparkled in his black curls.

Sophie blocked the doorway as well as she could, barring his entrance with a sense of futility. "Go away, Jason," she whispered, barely able to speak at all. "I don't want you here."

He pushed her ungently to one side and stepped in, closing the door behind him. "Is this the way you welcome all your guests?" he asked sardonically. He dropped the suitcase, going into the living room, and Sophie had to follow. He glanced curiously about the room, shrugging off his jacket. "Not bad," he commented.

Sophie found her voice and, by an effort of will, kept it steady. "I suppose you've come about a divorce. Why did you have to come here? You could have mailed the papers and I would have signed them. We have nothing to discuss."

Jason turned and fixed her with a penetrating stare of those dark eyes. "And I say we have plenty to discuss," he stated. "But not about a divorce. I don't want one, and I can't get rid of the feeling that you don't, either. Of course, this constant running away of yours will have to stop."

Sophie was recovering her equilibrium. "It won't happen again. I'm not coming back to live with you."

He raked one hand distractedly through his hair as he sat down abruptly on the sofa. "I wouldn't mind a glass of milk to settle my stomach." He grimaced in distaste. "That plastic airplane food."

Years of ingrained hospitality made it impossible for Sophie to refuse this simple request. When she returned from the kitchen with the cold milk, Jason was leaning back against the cushions, eyes closed, his long legs stretched out in front of him. Sophie suddenly realized that he was much more casually dressed than usual. He was wearing a blue cotton shirt and faded blue jeans, not at all what one expected of the successful executive.

He looked tired, his face drawn into strained lines with dark smudges beneath his eyes. Feeling a faint stirring of sympathy, she quelled it firmly. He would not get around her this time.

With catlike instinct he sensed her presence and opened his eyes. They were darkly shadowed, and for a second he seemed not to know where he was. Then they cleared. He took the glass of milk from her and, with a murmured thanks, drank half of it at one swallow, then wiped his mouth with the back of his hand. Putting the glass on the table, he looked across at her, his hard face totally impassive.

Sophie perched on the edge of an armchair, twisting her fingers nervously in her lap, waiting for him to speak.

"Why did you go, Sophie?" Jason said at last. "You knew we had to talk."

"You didn't stop me."

"I was at the factory about the accident."

"Is that cleared up?"

The corner of his mouth lifted. "Are you kidding? No, there's a bunch of insurance investigators looking into it, but it wasn't our negligence. Paul can handle it."

"What about the injured man?" Sophie asked.

"He'll be all right."

There was a short silence, during which Sophie fidgeted restlessly. "You didn't come all the way here to tell me that, did you?"

"No," he said quietly. "I came to ask you to come back to me. Now that I've arranged my business so it can practically run itself, I have plenty of time to persuade you, court you all over again if necessary."

Sophie's heart ached. He had come after her, but nothing had changed. He sounded as arrogant as ever. "What about Helen?"

Jason looked surprised. "What about her?" He gave a short, humorless laugh. "In case you're wondering, she admitted she lied about the baby. But I'd already decided to come here. Strange, when I met her in the hall with my suitcase, she turned white as if she'd faint. She asked where I was going. When I told her, she got this peculiar expression on her face, and then she said she was sorry she'd caused trouble for us. She wished me luck."

So Helen had finally admitted defeat. The knowledge gave Sophie little satisfaction, for she now realized that the relationship between Helen and Jason had been a product of Helen's imagination and her own mistrust of Jason. However, she reminded herself, Jason wasn't blameless in their own fiasco of a marriage.

"How generous of her," she said. "But you still believed her story about the baby, rather than mine. You didn't trust me. You're only here now because she told you the truth. Lack of trust is hardly a basis for a happy marriage." Her voice rose as pain knifed through her. "How could you believe for even one second that I would purposefully hurt a baby we made together?"

For a moment, Jason's face twisted with anguish, then he seemed to get hold of himself. He stared at her, his eyes black and tormented. "I didn't, Sophie." His hands came up to cover his face. "Well, I did, for a moment. But only because it was such a shock. After our week together I had such hopes for us. Then everything fell apart. I thought you hated me so much you'd gotten rid of the baby. I couldn't see anything but the pain that tore through me."

"I told you the truth," Sophie said dully. "It really was an accident. My baby," she added softly in a voice ragged with remembered pain, the unbearable loss of part of herself. And of Jason.

"I can't tell you how sorry I am, Sophie," Jason said gently. "The worst was knowing that you could have died. Why didn't you tell me you were going to have a baby? I would have come and taken care of you. We could have settled our differences. The baby would have been an interest for you."

"Is that how you see me, as a bearer of your children and the mistress of your house?" Sophie asked cynically, the first part of his statement failing completely to register in her brain until much later. "Didn't you ever see me as a person?"

Jason rose to his feet and began pacing distractedly about, his height dwarfing the room, reminding Sophie again of a jungle cat confined in a too-small cage. "Of course I saw you as a person. But what did you ever give of yourself? You calmly agreed to our marriage. You never asked me about my work, you never questioned me about anything I did except to complain when the novelty wore off your new toys. Toys I bought you, I might add," he finished with some of his best sarcasm.

"You never let me feel I could ask you about your life away from me," Sophie said, wounded. "You shut me out."

"I shut you out?" he said incredulously. "You shut me out." He turned toward her with a jerky movement. "Why didn't you ever dress like that in Greece?"

Astonished at the lightning change in subject, Sophie looked down at the ancient sweat shirt and old jeans, faded and shrunken so that they fit as snugly and comfortably as a second skin. "I thought you expected me to dress the part of a rich man's wife," she said in surprise.

"You didn't have to dress up all the time. You might have been a little more casual, more approachable."

Sophie felt like laughing, but there was no sign of humor in his face. The mighty Jason had thought her unapproachable? She could not meet the piercing gaze of his dark blue eyes, and she stared down at her hands folded in her lap.

"When I met you," Jason went on musingly, "I liked that air of aloofness you had, the elegance of your appearance. You were like a princess. But it began to get on my nerves. When there were only the two of us, couldn't you have relaxed more, gotten a little dusty and untidy? I began to think you didn't even sweat."

"Oh, I did," said Sophie dryly. "Especially when you started staying out all night."

Jason again raked his fingers through his hair. "You were used to having luxuries, used to buying everything you wanted. I had to work those long hours to make enough money so you'd never feel deprived or sorry you married me. At the same time I was angry that you behaved like a spoiled child, and we often fought when I came home. After a while it was easier to avoid you by sleeping at the office."

"Jason," Sophie protested. "If only you'd told me. I didn't need all those things. I only did it to make you notice me, like the child you called me. Sometimes you didn't even seem to know I was around, and I wondered why you even married me." She groaned inwardly. How shallow she'd been then. Thinking to redeem herself somehow, she said, "But we had our good times too, didn't we?"

Breaking off in mid-stride, Jason reseated himself. He half smiled. "Yes, we had good times, too. Mostly in bed."

Sophie's face flamed scarlet, yet she know it was true. In bed they had been good. It had been their only real communication.

Jason spoke again. "And last week was good, too." He arose and came toward her. "Sophie, we've both changed. Let's try again. We won't make the same mistakes twice, and we'll have the good times better than before."

Sophie quickly got up and moved away from her chair, putting the width of the room between them. "No, Jason. You have a powerful weapon there, but it won't work this time." She went swiftly to the window and, drawing aside the curtain, looked out into the night, her arms hugging her stomach. Sheets of rain hung silver in the light of street lamps, and the road glistened blackly.

Jason came up behind her and wrapped his arms around her, his hands covering hers. He laid his face against the silky fall of her hair. "Why did you ever go?" he murmured. She knew it wasn't only for the last time that he questioned her, but also for the first time. "I want you to come back. I want you to be my wife again. Maybe if I say it often enough, you'll believe me.''

She struggled weakly to free herself. His scent was drugging her will, and lethargy seeped dangerously into her bones. He pressed closer. She could not ignore the fact that his desire was awakening, his body growing and hardening against hers.

But his time there was no moon madness to blind her reason, to seduce her senses. "I can't," she managed to say. "It'll be like before, and I couldn't bear that."

"I want you, Sophie," Jason repeated, sounding desperate and strangely disheartened—or was it her imagination, dreaming meaning into his words that she wished to put there. Surely it couldn't mean that much to him.

She freed herself and moved to the center of the room. Jason let the curtain fall. "Sophie—" he began again.

She interrupted hotly, "You want me, Jason. Always you want me. But wanting is not enough. It's never enough." Her voice broke and she sat down, covering her face with her hands as hot tears burned her eyes.

As if from a long distance she heard his low voice, "Would it be enough if I said I love you?"

Incredulous, she lowered her hands. Her gray eyes searched his face, but she could detect no deceit in his set features. Was he sincere? Or was this just another ploy to satisfy his possessiveness, his need to own her?

She couldn't believe him. She was too afraid that another betrayal would cost her her sanity. She said, her eyes fixed on the floor, "It's too late. Nothing has changed. We don't understand each other in the most basic areas."

She dared not look up for fear of what she would see in his face. The silence hung between them like a dark, heavy blanket. Then Jason spoke again, his back to her, "Sophie, I need you. Please—don't send me away." The raw anguish in his voice tore at her heart, and her overpowering love for him overcame her fears.

She rushed to him and threw herself at his feet, her arms around his knees. "Jason, stay," she cried from her soul. "I love you."

He drew her to her feet and led her to the sofa where he sat down, pulling her down with him so that she lay in his arms. He began to kiss her with deep, sensual kisses filled with longing and yearning and sorrow for the length of time it had taken them to reach this point where all the barriers were down. Sophie returned them rapturously, her face wet with tears.

When Jason paused to drag a ragged breath into his lungs, she looked into his face and saw that some of the tears were not her own, but his. "Jason," she murmured, her hands in his hair pulling him down to her again. "Dear Jason."

A harsh sob shook him. "Sophie, we've wasted so much time." The words came out jerkily, almost incoherently. "Us, the baby. Can it all be put right? Is it really too late?" He clutched her convulsively. "Oh, Sophie, hold me."

"I'm holding you, Jason," she whispered, her heart so full she could hardly speak.

"You will come back with me, Sophie?" he muttered thickly, his mouth against her throat.

"Yes, my Jason, my only love. I'll come with you, to the ends of the earth if that's what you want." She held him tightly, as if she would never let him go. "It's been so lonely without you."

"For me, too. But never again." He raised his head to look at her, and the love in his eyes started fresh tears flowing down her cheeks. He brushed them away with a gentle finger. "We'll go back to Greece, to the endless sunshine. But we'll come here sometimes too, so you can see your friend Laura, and so our children will know their mother's country."

A shadow crossed Sophie's face. Jason saw it and instantly knew its cause. "My darling," he said with deep understanding. "I know what you feel. We could have had a son." He gave her a little shake, dropping a kiss on her nose. "We'll have our children, and I'll be with you all the way."

Any remaining guilt she felt drained away. He understood her loss, and he no longer blamed her. "I know, Jason," she murmured, her mind's eye seeing a little boy and a little girl with Jason's dark eyes, filled with the laughter she hoped would light his more often now. "Stavros will be so happy. He'll act like he planned the whole thing when we come home together."

"Stavros." Jason grinned, hugging her more tightly. "Sometimes I think you married me only to be related to him." He sobered for an instant. "What about the shop? Will you mind leaving it?"

She shook her head. "Laura can run the shop on her own. I know she'd like to. I can always open one in Athens."

Jason laughed. "As I suggested this summer."

She smiled at him fondly. "As you suggested. It'll be a challenge, and I'll be close to you."

She turned up her face, parting her mouth in expectation of his kiss, her face filled with love and passionate desire to be truly one with him. The laughter faded from Jason's face as he saw the openness, the trust, in her beautiful features. "Jason," she whispered. "Kiss me. Oh, kiss me."

"Darling—" The rest of his exclamation was smothered against her trembling mouth. He raised his head after a moment and looked deep into her clear gray eyes. "Where is your bedroom?" he whispered huskily.

Speechless, Sophie gestured down the hall. Jason stood up with her in his arms and strode to the bedroom. She could feel the tension in him, the tension of a man who has waited all his life and can wait no longer. She was momentarily afraid of the hunger in him, but only for an instant. He had the power to create a hunger in her that would match his own.

They made love with delectable slowness, savoring each kiss and every caress, as if they were lovers meeting for the first time, or the last time. But underneath Jason's control, his ability to postpone his satisfaction in order to fully satisfy hers, Sophie sensed a desperate need and raw hunger that had never been there before. Even in Kalamata, there had at times been an anger in his lovemaking, a desire to punish her. Now there was only mounting passion and an overwhelming love.

"Jason," she cried. "I love you," and arched herself to meet the urgency of his body. He took her fiercely and groaned her name as together they shared an ecstatic fulfillment.

They came down slowly and reluctantly. Sophie opened her eyes and saw that the rain was still whispering against the window as softly as a love song. Beautiful music, she thought drowsily, like Jason's love.

Her thoughts lost their coherence and she slept, clasped tightly in Jason's arms, against the whole warm length of him, as she would all the nights of her life.

The church was empty, a vast peaceful cavern, smelling faintly of incense and burned wax.

They both knelt, praying silently—for their future, for the child who had almost been theirs, for the children they would yet have. As if by telepathy, they raised their heads at the same time, looking deep into each other's eyes, communicating their profound love and lasting, unbreakable commitment to each other.

"We'll never be apart again," Jason said, holding both hands out to her.

"No, we'll always be together," Sophie said with a tender smile as she took his hands.

He bent his head and softly kissed her palms, first one and then the other. "Promise?" he asked.

"I promise," she said solemnly. "Jason, I love you."

"And I love you, my Sophie."

Silhouette Desire

COMING NEXT MONTH

GOLDEN GODDESS
Stephanie James

What right did Jarrett have to demand her love? He
was the wrong kind of man, with his fanatical
interest in primitive art and antiquated ideas about
women. But could Hannah be wrong, and Jarrett be
Mr Right...?

RIVER OF DREAMS
Naomi Horton

Even as Leigh reveled in his arms she knew she
couldn't afford the commitment he demanded.
Soon she'd have to choose... before the perilous
cruise had run its course.

TO HAVE IT ALL
Robin Elliot

Brant's reputation preceded him, and Jenna had her
doubts about getting involved. He said he wanted
them to have it all, but Jenna had more in mind than
Oreo cookies and a pet Canary.

COMING NEXT MONTH

LEADER OF THE PACK
Diana Stuart

Weylin Matthews made Jenna's dogs bark as though
a wolf had walked into the camp. He seemed to have
some mysterious power over her . . . When she
looked into his eyes, she could refuse him nothing.

FALSE IMPRESSIONS
Ariel Berk

Brandon Fox didn't look like a typical girlie-joint
customer — he was the handsomest man Audrey had
ever seen — but he was there. And ogling was the
word that certainly sprang to mind, since he couldn't
seem to take his eyes off her. But first impressions are
often false . . .

WINTER MEETING
Doreen Owens Malek

Leda knew Reardon was the one man she should
avoid at all costs. But one glimpse of the pain and
determination in his bleak gray eyes told her he was
also the one man she could never turn away from.

Rebecca had set herself on course for loneliness and despair. It took a plane crash and a struggle to survive in the wilds of the Canadian Northwest Territories to make her change – and to let her fall in love with the only other survivor, handsome Guy McLaren.

Arctic Rose is her story – and you can read it from the 14th February for just £2.25.

The story continues with Rebecca's sister, Tamara, available soon.

Silhouette Desire Romances

TAKE 4
THRILLING SILHOUETTE
DESIRE ROMANCES
ABSOLUTELY FREE

Experience all the excitement, passion and pure joy of love. Discover fascinating stories brought to you by Silhouette's top selling authors. At last an opportunity for you to become a regular reader of Silhouette Desire. You can enjoy 6 superb new titles every month from Silhouette Reader Service, with a whole range of special benefits, a free monthly Newsletter packed with recipes, competitions and exclusive book offers. Plus information on the top Silhouette authors, a monthly guide to the stars and extra bargain offers.

An Introductory FREE GIFT for YOU.
Turn over the page for details.

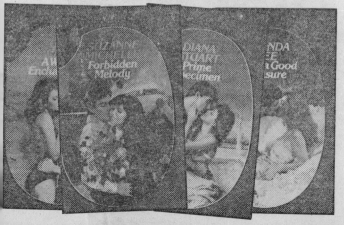

As a special introduction we will send you FOUR
specially selected Silhouette Desire romances
— yours to keep FREE — when you complete
and return this coupon to us.

At the same time, because we believe that you will be so thrilled
with these novels, we will reserve a subscription to Silhouette
Reader Service for you. Every month you will receive 6 of the very
latest novels by leading romantic fiction authors, delivered direct to
your door.

Postage and packing is always completely
free. There is no obligation or commitment —
you can cancel your subscription at any time.

It's so easy. Send no money now. Simply fill in and post
the coupon today to:-

**SILHOUETTE READER SERVICE, FREEPOST,
P.O. Box 236 Croydon, SURREY CR9 9EL**

Please note: READERS IN SOUTH AFRICA to write to:-
Silhouette, Postbag X3010 Randburg 2125 S. Africa

FREE BOOKS CERTIFICATE

**To: Silhouette Reader Service, FREEPOST, PO Box 236,
Croydon, Surrey CR9 9EL**

Please send me, Free and without obligation, four specially selected Silhouette Desire Romances and reserve a
Reader Service Subscription for me. If I decide to subscribe, I shall, from the beginning of the month following my
free parcel of books, receive six books each month for £5.94, post and packing free. If I decide not to subscribe I
shall write to you within 10 days. The free books are mine to keep in any case. I understand that I may cancel my
subscription at any time simply by writing to you. I am over 18 years of age.
Please write in BLOCK CAPITALS.

Name _____

Address _____

_____

_____ Postcode _____

SEND NO MONEY — TAKE NO RISKS
*Remember postcodes speed delivery. Offer applies in U.K. only
and is not valid to present subscribers. Silhouette reserve the right
to exercise discretion in granting membership. If price changes
are necessary you will be notified.
Offer limited to one per household. Offer expires April 30th, 1986.*

EP18SD